"What am I doing? I'm seducing you..."

Gabriel slid his fingers through the long sweep of Tessa's hair, enjoying the silky thickness. "You've finally admitted this attraction we've got going on here. It's time to see how far we can push it. How long we can play it out."

"Oh, I'll bet you're good for at least a few long, hard hours," she said in a husky tone, her fingers tiptoeing up his chest, leaving hot little trails.

"Oh, yeah, I could keep you panting and wet for hours," he promised, leaning closer as if to kiss her. At the last second, he shifted so his lips brushed the softest whisper over her cheek. "But we could do better than that."

Her breath hitched a little, her gaze blurred with pleasure. The fingers of both her hands were kneading his chest, nails digging in gently in a sexy rhythm that promised a superb sense of timing.

Gabe knew his limits, knew how far he could push this desire before he hit the point of no return.

Now to find out hers.

And, in a flash as powerful as his spiking desire, he realized what she was doing.

She wanted to spike this heat, accelerate it so it blew, hot, fast and furious. Then she'd turn on those sexy heels of hers and walk away without a glance.

Gabriel understood her strategy. He even admired it.

But it wasn't going to happen...

Dear Reader,

Ahh, weddings. Don't you love them? Since they are often the end result in a romance novel, I'm a big fan. But the wedding preparation? Oh, man, talk about stress! Especially when the bride keeps changing her mind. Which is why in *A SEAL's Pleasure*, Tessa's best friend's wedding has become her biggest nightmare. For a woman used to speaking her mind and going after what she wants, simply smiling and going along is pushing the bounds of friendship.

Which made it even more fun to give Tessa a delicious distraction like Gabriel, aka Romeo to his SEAL team (a worthy nickname, as many a woman will attest). Not only is Gabriel gorgeous, sexy and fun, he challenges Tessa to learn what romance is. Pretty fitting for a wedding, right?

I hope you enjoy *A SEAL's Pleasure* and that you'll check out the rest of my sexy SEAL series. You can find them on my website, as well as insider peeks into this story and others. Visit tawnyweber.com or find me at facebook.com/tawnyweber.romanceauthor or follow me on Twitter @TawnyWeber.

Happy reading,

Tawny Weber

New York Times Bestselling Author

Tawny Weber

———

A SEAL's Pleasure

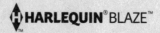

HARLEQUIN® BLAZE™

Recycling programs
for this product may
not exist in your area.

ISBN-13: 978-0-373-79847-6

A SEAL's Pleasure

Printed in U.S.A.

www.Harlequin.com

A *New York Times* and *USA TODAY* bestselling author of over thirty hot books, **Tawny Weber** has been writing sassy, sexy romances since her first Harlequin Blaze book was published in 2007. A fan of Johnny Depp, cupcakes and color coordination, she spends a lot of her time shopping for cute shoes, scrapbooking and hanging out on Facebook.

Readers can check out Tawny's books at her website, tawnyweber.com, or join her Red Hot Readers Club for goodies such as free reads, complete first-chapter excerpts, recipes, insider story info and much more. Look for her on Facebook at facebook.com/tawnyweber. romanceauthor and follow her on Twitter @TawnyWeber.

Books by Tawny Weber

HARLEQUIN BLAZE

Blazing Bedtime Stories, Volume VII
"Wild Thing"
Nice & Naughty
Midnight Special
Naughty Christmas Nights

Uniformly Hot!

A SEAL's Seduction
A SEAL's Surrender
A SEAL's Salvation
A SEAL's Kiss
A SEAL's Fantasy
Christmas with a SEAL
A SEAL's Secret

COSMO RED-HOT READS FROM HARLEQUIN

Fearless

To get the inside scoop on Harlequin Blaze and its talented writers, be sure to check out blazeauthors.com.

All backlist available in ebook format.

Visit the Author Profile page at Harlequin.com for more titles

To all of the bridesmaids, everywhere!

1

CHIEF PETTY OFFICER Gabriel Thorne had yet to find a challenge he couldn't meet, beat or defeat.

And today's game was no different.

Ignoring the noise, the intense stares and the heavy expectations, he assessed the field, making note of all of his options even as his mind calculated risks and probabilities. There were three easy shots, ones that would assure him an advance. But Gabriel had no need for easy.

A quick glance at the clock assured him that he did have a need for speed, though.

He leaned over the pool table, slid the cue between his fingers and, in a practiced move, placed a machine-gun shot right in the center of the waiting balls, sending them all flying home to clear the table.

"And that's how it's done," he told his scowling opponent.

Gabriel easily read the fury in the guy's face, but kept his grin in check while the other man yanked his wallet from his slacks pocket.

"Another round," insisted Jase Jeglinski—otherwise known as Jackrabbit to the SEAL team.

"Another time." Gabriel tilted his chin toward the billiard-ball-shaped clock on the wall, ignoring the mutinous set of Jackrabbit's jaw and the guy's clenched fists.

Even if he'd let one fly, Gabriel would have reacted with the same easy disregard. Because there was nothing Jackrabbit could dish out that Gabriel couldn't take.

The easy confidence he'd been born with had been carefully honed to a razor-sharp edge in his years in the military.

"Dude, do you ever lose?" another of the men surrounding them asked in awe.

"Romeo? Never." Scavenger laughed as he collected his own winnings from the other three men. "I warned you not to bet against him."

Gabriel shook his head. Leave it to Scavenger—aka Petty Officer Shane O'Brian to anyone not on the SEAL team—to make sure the odds were as even and fair as possible. Sooner or later, he'd learn that it didn't matter what he did—life just wasn't gonna turn out fair. But Gabriel figured it was his job to watch his buddy's back, not to offer up that particular lesson.

"You keep him around to carry your ego?" Jackrabbit asked with a laugh that held no amusement as Scavenger expanded his praise to include Gabriel's legendary success with the ladies.

"Nah. I keep him around because he can turn a tin can, a pile of sand and a couple of rocks into a tactical communications device that will get our ass out from behind enemy lines," Gabriel retorted, only half joking since he was sure the communications specialist could do just that.

He ignored Jackrabbit's skeptical snort because he understood it. A SEAL team wasn't a team simply because the group of men had been assigned together. They had to work together and prove themselves to establish real trust.

Gabriel, or Romeo as he was more often referred to, Scavenger and their pal Irish, aka Mitch Donovan, had been reassigned from Virginia to the West Coast less than seven months ago and had been otherwise deployed for most of that time. So while they were a part of the team on paper, until they'd deployed on a mission with the rest of the men, he knew they were still proving themselves.

"So that's the shooting range, the pool table and what was the other one?" Tall and dark haired with a muscular build that leaned toward lanky, Lt. Taylor Powell gave Jackrabbit an amused look. "Beer guzzling, wasn't it?"

"He can't win them all."

"Sure he can," Scavenger disagreed with a friendly smile. "I've never seen him lose a bet."

"All that means is he only takes sure bets," Jackrabbit said with a growl, obviously still pissed.

Gabriel didn't blame him. Losing sucked. Or so he'd heard.

"Ops, bets, women," Scavenger said in a musing sort of tone. "We've served together for six years now and I'm pretty sure he's won them all."

To prove his point, he continued regaling the others with a few of Gabriel's exploits.

Gabriel ignored the stories and the ensuing laughter as he racked up the balls for whoever wanted to play the next round. He didn't need to defend himself. His record stood solid on its own. Jackrabbit would see that soon enough, since they were heading into training together next week.

He'd learn that Gabriel was used to winning.

Define your path, stand your ground. That was what his grandfather had taught him. That and to never let anyone else's actions define his own. Simple rules that'd defined his life. Because of them, he'd survived leaving the reservation and living on the streets after his grandfather died. He'd got out of the slums, he'd joined the Navy, he'd become a SEAL. Because of those rules, he'd never met a challenge he couldn't meet, beat or defeat.

It was what he did.

It was who he was.

Maybe it hadn't always been that way, but it was now. And now was all that mattered.

Gabriel glanced at the clock again, noting how fast time was flying by.

"C'mon, boys. We've got a party to get to."

Not that Irish would be docking points for them being late to his little shindig. But Gabriel figured their commander's bride-to-be might be a little put out if half of her fiancé's team was late to their engagement celebration. And Gabriel made a point to never disappoint a lady.

As one, the eight men strode out of Olive Oyl's bar with a wave here and a shout-out there to familiar faces. Outside, the cool air washed over them in welcome as they straddled their motorcycles. Not nearly as comfortable as they'd be in jeans or even in uniform, some of the men tucked their ties into their shirts, a couple of them stowing their suit jackets into their saddlebags.

Gabriel, who hadn't bothered to put either on yet, simply unhooked his helmet. Before he could pull it on, the deceptively lanky guy on the Indian Chief next to him tilted his head.

"Watch your back," murmured Mr. Wizard, as the team called Taylor. "Jackrabbit's got a hard-on to take you down."

"Ain't gonna happen."

"He's just superstitious," Scavenger remarked from the other side, his words pitched low enough that nobody beyond the three of them could hear over the roaring engines. "He figures your luck has to run out eventually and he doesn't want to be on a mission with you when it does."

Scavenger really believed that? Damn, the guy was gullible. In the act of unlocking his helmet, Gabriel exchanged looks with Taylor, who was rolling his eyes.

"Jackrabbit can keep his hard-ons and his superstitions

to himself," Gabriel stated, pulling his helmet on to put an end to the conversation.

But as he kicked the Harley to life and put it into gear, Jackrabbit angled his bike into the lead, deliberately cutting off Gabriel. Forced to admit that Mr. Wizard had a point, Gabriel bided his time. As soon as they hit the freeway onramp, he throttled hard, letting the bike fly around traffic. He kept it just under one hundred miles per hour, not needing to look at the speedometer to confirm since he knew the bike as well as he knew his own body. All it took was a glance in the rearview mirror to assure him that the team had accepted his challenge.

And the race was on.

Grinning into the wind as it beat against his face, Gabriel took the scenic route—off the freeway, along the beach, through every twist and turn he could find. Might as well make it interesting.

By the time they'd caught up in the parking lot of the fancy renovated manor house, he'd wrapped himself in a tie, pulled on his suit jacket and was adjusting his cuffs.

Gabriel waited until everyone had dismounted and they were all ready to head in to the party before clapping Jackrabbit on the shoulder.

"Why don't you just accept it, bro? I always win."

TESSA MONROE EASILY ignored the appreciative looks and heated stares as she crossed the elegant ballroom surrounded by the glitter of crystal, the sweetness of white roses and the tinkling melody of good cheer.

Her long brunette curls swayed over milky white skin, the rich purple of her silky dress perfectly fitting the posh ambiance of the ballroom.

The setting suited her.

Of course, she looked just as good in the gym wearing

skimpy, yet breathable cotton. Or on the beach in a tiny bikini. On the slopes wearing layers, behind her laptop while she interviewed relationship experts for her latest column or on a date with the latest in her string of male conquests.

Simply put, she was a woman used to being admired.

So used to it that she barely noticed. Instead, she admired the huge manor. Lit up like a beacon, the chandeliers glinted as music played softly in the background. The ballroom was so filled with people that Tessa welcomed the cool March night air wafting through the open doors. She could see the torch-lit paths leading from the gardens to the beach beyond, but didn't think anyone had ventured out yet.

It was a lovely party that suited Olivia Kane perfectly. And Tessa wanted her best friend to be safe and happy. But Livi was making a huge mistake. Tessa knew it; she was terrified of it. Yet she couldn't do a damned thing about it. Not without putting her friend's happiness—and more important, her health—at risk.

So Tessa did something so unusual, so out of character, that she had to focus on it with all her being. She ignored her instincts, put aside her personal prejudices and, God forbid it became a habit, for the first time in her life she tried faking it.

With her brightest smile plastered on her face, she pretended she was perfectly thrilled as she made her way to her dearest, oldest friend's side to celebrate what could be a huge, painful mistake.

Marriage.

Tessa shuddered.

She had to say something. At least get Livi to consider what she was jumping into. Not just marriage. But marriage to a military man. A SEAL.

Her mind simply boggled.

"Livi…" Her voice trailed off as the rest of the words disappeared somewhere in her throat before they reached her tongue.

"Yes?"

Her blond hair twisted into a cascading crown of curls down the shoulder of her lipstick-red dress and her huge brown eyes dancing with happiness, Livi looked better than Tessa had ever seen her. Tucking her arm into Tessa's, Livi offered a bright smile, hers as genuine as the sweetness shining from her face.

How the two of them were such good friends was baffling, since the only thing sweet about Tessa was her taste in desserts.

"About all of this," Tessa said, waving her hand to indicate the party. But once more her words trailed off as she looked into Livi's face.

She glowed, as if she were lit from within with happiness. Joy shone in Livi's eyes, pleasure curved her lips and her entire being simply radiated delight.

Crap. Tessa sighed. She couldn't do it.

"Can I get you more cider?" she offered instead, gesturing to Livi's almost empty glass with her own champagne flute.

"Oh, no. I'm fine. Isn't it lovely here?" Practically bouncing in her Louboutin shoes, Livi gazed around the beachside manor. "I'd so love to have the wedding here, but there aren't spots available until November."

Before Tessa could suggest she hold out, since November was only eight months away—didn't it take years to plan these sorts of things anyway?—Livi continued.

"But obviously we can't wait that long," she said with a soft laugh. Rubbing her hand over her silk-covered, flat belly, she added, "Mitch's mother would really like it better if we were married before the baby arrives."

And that settled it.

Tessa offered a passing waiter a smile big enough to make him trip in his rush to bring her another glass of champagne. As soon as she'd exchanged flutes, she knocked back half of the bubbly to hide her grimace.

"Now, that's a sight made to make women swoon," Livi murmured with an appreciative sigh. "You know, we work with good-looking, incredibly built men all the time, but these guys give new meaning to the word *fit.*"

Ready to be distracted, Tessa put her worries aside. Because if there were one thing she made a point of appreciating on a regular basis, it was men. So much so that she'd managed to turn her enjoyment of the male species into a career writing about the games between the sexes.

Sometimes when she was alone late at night she wondered how long she could finesse her talent for flirting into a viable profession. When the clock ran out on that option, what would she do? Emulate her mother, who'd flirted her way through six—and counting—marriages so far?

Tessa shuddered at the thought.

More than ready to be distracted and play, Tessa followed her friend's gaze in search of a worthy opponent.

And damn near spun on her five-inch Giuseppe Zanotti heels and ran the other way.

Her heart skipped, bouncing in her chest a few times before plunging into her stomach. It had plenty of company there, as it tangled up with a wild jangle of anticipation, nerves and lust. She tried to swallow but her throat was too dry. Her tongue, usually quite nimble, was glued to the roof of her mouth.

She shifted her gaze to the gardens beyond the French doors, pretending she found the sight peaceful. Fingers clenching and unclenching around the stem of her glass, she took a couple of deep breaths and focused on pulling the soothing air down to her belly until she found some semblance of calm.

Then she looked back at the group of men who'd just walked into the mansion.

Her heart raced again. Emotions spun through her, too fast to identify. It didn't matter. She didn't care what they were. Only that they spun right back out.

"Why is he…they here?" she asked, hoping Livi hadn't caught her slip of the tongue.

"The team? You don't think Mitch would celebrate our engagement without his SEALs, do you?" Livi asked with a laugh. Then, before Tessa realized what her friend was going to do so she could have grabbed her arm to stop her, Livi gave a big ol' exuberant wave.

As one, the men looked their way.

But Tessa only saw one man.

Taller than the rest, his shoulders broad and tempting beneath a lightweight sport coat the same vivid black as his eyes, he wore a simple dress shirt under his jacket, yet managed to look perfectly elegant.

His gaze locked on her, sending a zing of desire through her body with the same intensity as it had the first time he'd looked her way six months before.

Tessa Monroe, the woman who'd flicked off movie stars, who'd written articles calling out misogynists and who always—always—came out on top when it came to any encounter with the opposite sex, wanted to duck behind her friend and hide.

"That's so sweet of his friends to come all this way to celebrate your engagement to Mitch," she said hopefully, watching Livi's fiancé stride through the crowd to greet the group with back slaps and what looked to be laughing taunts. "Isn't most of Mitch's team stationed across the country?"

"They didn't have to come far. They're all based in Coronado now. Didn't I tell you?" Livi asked, her eyes locked on Mitch as if she could eat him up with her gaze alone. "Romeo's the best man."

Romeo.

Tessa's smile dropped away as dread and something else curled low in her belly.

Her gaze cut across the room, honing in on the man she'd secretly dubbed her personal kryptonite after just one meeting. And had judiciously avoided ever since.

Gabriel Thorne. Aka Romeo.

His eyes were still locked on her.

At least a hundred feet separated them, but Tessa could see the heat in that midnight gaze.

It was as if he could look inside her mind and deep into her soul and see everything she'd hidden away. All of her desires, her every need, her secret wants.

A wicked smile angled over his chiseled face, assuring her that he not only saw them all, but that he was also quite sure that he could fulfill every single one. And in ways that would leave her panting, sweaty and begging for more.

There was very little Tessa didn't know about sex. She appreciated the act, reveled in the results and had long ago mastered the ins and outs of, well, in and out. She knew how to use sex, how to enjoy sex and how to avoid sex.

So if anyone had told her that she'd feel a low, needy promise of an orgasm curling tight in her belly from just a single look across a crowded room, she'd have given their cheek a pitying pat and laughed at them.

And now, she admitted to herself, she'd have had to apologize for her mistake.

"Shall we?" Livi murmured, making as if to hurry across the room.

"I'll catch up later," Tessa promised. At Livi's frown,

she added, "I want to check with your mother and make sure everything is on schedule. You know, maid-of-honor stuff."

"Willingly seek out Pauline, who you know perfectly well has everything under control?" Livi's frown deepened as she planted her fists on her hips. "What's going on?"

Over Livi's shoulder, Tessa could see the men starting to make their way through the crowd toward them. Something clenched tight in her belly and it took her a second to identify it as panic. Desperate to get away but still not willing to upset Livi, her mind raced for an out. Wetting her lips, she shifted her smile from friendly to sultry and leaned toward her friend in a confiding way.

"There's a very yummy model here I've been wanting a taste of ever since I saw how he could hold up a pair of jeans with his *stuff* alone. He's over by the buffet," she murmured. "You play hostess. I'm going to get a nibble before someone else dishes him up."

"Stuff?" Livi's laugh pealed with delight, her quick hug filling Tessa with enough guilt that she told herself she'd find a model somewhere tonight to flirt with. "Go, taste, nibble, enjoy. Just remember you have to sit at the head table for dinner."

The head table. With the bride- and groom-to-be, and most likely their erstwhile best man.

Tessa offered a weak smile.

It was enough to make a girl lose her appetite.

WELL, WELL.

When a party was thrown by a woman who made her living as a fitness trainer, the guests were bound to be hot and gorgeous, with bodies to match. And Livi's party proved that Southern California had a vast variety of gorgeous to choose from.

But Gabriel's body hummed for just one particular woman. Petite perfection, Tessa Monroe was like something out of a dream. A very wet, sweaty, lust-filled dream. With long dark hair that called to a man's more prurient fantasies and a face made for bad poetry and deep sighs, she was gorgeous even from across the room. Wrapped in a tiny bit of purple silk, her body was fifty shades of amazing, with curves and angles that promised almost more than a mere man could handle. *Almost.*

Gabriel had no doubts about his ability to handle her. But he was getting impatient. He'd been waiting to get his shot at the sexy little angel for more months than he cared to admit. And tonight was it. His chance to finally start making good on every hot dream he'd had about Miss Tessa Monroe since their first meeting last Halloween.

He'd never figured out why she'd taken an instant dislike to him. He hadn't gotten further than introductions that night before she'd shot him down. A first, and not one he cared to repeat. Gabriel still didn't know what'd caused her instant animosity. His cologne? His Native American brave costume? A hideous past life experience where he'd kidnapped her from her wagon-train adventure, carried her off into the woods and introduced her to the carnal delights of the flesh?

Whatever it was, it was standing in the way of all the great sex they should be having. And tonight was the night to see it gone.

Even as he exchanged greetings with Mitch, clapped hands with his friend's father, Captain Donovan, and shared friendly nods with various brass surrounding them, Gabriel watched Tessa flee. She'd probably claim that she was simply showing her disinterest in his presence. But he'd seen the look in her eyes. That flash of desire so hot it came with a mind-blowing guarantee. The dismay, reluctance and anger that had followed told him she wasn't quite ready to see that guarantee through, though.

Not yet.

Rocking back on his heels, he assured himself that it wouldn't take much to push her over.

"Gabriel."

His smile shifting from predatory to friendly, he opened his arms to Livi, giving her a gentle hug. She was a total sweetheart and it was easy to see why his friend had fallen for her. Gabriel was still having trouble with the concept of Mitch actually marrying—some things just didn't mix. Oil and water, fire and ice, military and marriage. Hence Gabriel's relationship rule—keep it light and easy, walk away early, leave them with a smile. He'd never ask a woman to make the sacrifices necessary to be with a military man, and he refused to let any woman be a distraction from his number one focus—his career.

But that was him. Irish was different. So even knowing his friend was probably making a mistake, Gabriel still understood the motivation behind his friend's decision. Irish was gonna be a dad, so this was the right thing to do. And Irish was nothing if not right.

And lucky, given that his baby momma was a doll like Livi.

"You're gorgeous," he told her in greeting.

"I was just going to say the same thing to you," she said with a soft laugh. "How do you get better looking every time I see you?"

"Clean living and fresh sea air," he joked, since he'd spent a large part of the past three months on an aircraft carrier. "How about you? Don't tell me it's Irish that's put the glow in your smile."

"In my smile, in my heart," Livi murmured with a sheepish grin.

Her gaze cut to Mitch, and Gabriel had to admit, the emotions shining in those eyes were enough to make him wish for a second that he believed in marriage. Because if anyone deserved a happy one, it was the pretty blonde and his best pal.

"Enough with this guy," Mitch said as he joined them. "He already knows how fabulous you are. Ready to meet the rest of the team so they can know, too?"

Gabriel saw the nerves in Livi's eyes, felt her take a bracing breath and knew she was battling her instinctive shyness as she was introduced to the large group of men. What must that be like? Gabriel wondered. Not shyness. That was a concept so beyond his comprehension that it wasn't even worth considering.

But the idea of having a woman put her own fears, her own issues, aside for you… Gabriel was used to women wanting to do a lot of things with his body, and there were just as many who'd be happy to lay claim to his emotions. But he'd never known a single one—his own mother included—who gave a damn enough to put him ahead of anything in their little world.

Once the introductions were through and everyone had offered their wishes, Mitch tilted his head toward the room, indicating the men were on their own. Livi, easily reading him, offered to take the team around and introduce them.

"We're fine," Gabriel assured her. "I'm sure we'll find plenty to entertain ourselves."

And so they did.

By the time the team meandered through the party, exchanged greetings, snagged beers and commandeered a table in the back, Gabriel had plenty of entertaining options.

What he didn't have, though, was a clue as to where his quarry had scurried. Because as intriguing as the many offers he'd received were, there was only one woman he was interested in tonight.

The only one who'd ever turned him down.

Tessa Monroe.

His very own angel.

2

SOME WOMEN ATE when they were stressed, and why not? Who didn't love the comfort of chocolate?

Others managed their stress by shopping. Because, well, one could never have too many pairs of shoes.

She'd used both tactics from time to time with varying degrees of success. But Tessa often said her favorite go-to guaranteed stress reliever was sex. It loosened the body, eased tension and, if done right—and she tended to do it right—emptied the mind of pesky thoughts and trouble-some worries.

But despite her reputation as a man-eater, it'd been a while since she'd had sex, stress relieving or otherwise.

Besides, all things considered—all things being that sex itself was integral to the stress dancing through her system—she'd hit her second-favorite release reliever.

The pool table.

Tessa leaned forward, angling from the waist as she peered down the pool cue and lined up her shot. She wasn't concerned with the minuscule length of her dress. Hey, she could feel the silky fabric against the back of her upper thighs. She knew she wasn't sharing anything she didn't want to. She never did.

Besides, the party was still confined to the main rooms of the manor. Guests likely wouldn't break away into small pockets until after dinner. She'd have regained her usual poise and control long before then.

"Two ball in the corner pocket," she murmured.

She had overreacted. A silly thing to do, and she was sure it was because she was worried about Livi. Maybe she was a little stressed because things were so crazy at the magazine right now, too. After a year of running around the country with Livi to promote one workout video after another, it was just weird to be home for so long actually working out of the *Flirtatious* offices instead of emailing her articles in.

She was just having a little trouble readjusting, getting back into the groove of her life.

That was why work was stressing her out.

Why she was getting all wiggy over seeing Thorne again.

That was all it was. Stress causing a little overreaction.

Because Tessa Monroe never, ever worried about a man.

A *man*. Tessa hissed between her teeth at the idea of a mere man shaking her confidence. It'd been months since she'd seen the guy. They'd only met the one time last Halloween and she'd taken an instant dislike. Not to the man himself, but to the power he seemed to have over her.

All he'd done was introduce himself and shake her hand on Halloween. His touch had sent a zing of desire through her, more potent than anything she'd ever felt in her life. With just that touch, she'd known he could take over her world. That he could bring her the most incredible pleasure, the wildest joy. And the deepest pain.

Something she refused to allow any man.

Yet here she was, hiding from him.

And all he'd done was flash his smile her way.

Ridiculous, she reminded herself as she watched the pretty white cue ball spin across the green felt. It smacked the blue ball with a loud crack, sending it in a fast diagonal slide into the corner pocket.

She'd overreacted earlier, like she had on Halloween.

Just because Gabriel Thorne looked as if he could see all the way into her soul and knew her every secret wish and dream didn't mean he really could. He might think she was going to fall at his feet simply by virtue of his gorgeous face and sexy body, but he was wrong. Tessa Monroe didn't fall for any man. Especially not one so used to stepping over the bodies of his groupies to welcome the next conquest.

Who cared if he was the sexiest man she'd ever met in her entire life? The promise of incredible sex would never be incentive enough to give any man the kind of power Gabriel demanded with a single look.

"Three in the side," she muttered through clenched teeth.

Hell, she made her living understanding the influence of sex appeal. The lure of engaging the opposite sex. The delight of flirtatious interplay. She was an expert. Well, sort of an expert.

At least expert enough to know that this…

She took a deep breath, trying to shake off the needy feelings clutched low in her belly as she attempted to put a name on whatever it was she felt.

This *thing* she was feeling for Thorne was just a chemical reaction. Not a big deal. After all, sexual sparks were as easy to come by as a good Wi-Fi connection. All it took was tapping in to the right signal, a password or a clever hack and voilà. A world of possibilities, right there at a girl's fingertips.

Tessa straightened, leaning on the pool cue as she inspected the table. The sound of laughter and chatter filtered through her focus, reminding her that the cocktail party was heating up in the rooms beyond. Figuring she had another three, maybe five minutes max before she'd be missed, Tessa bent low again, planted her feet in their five-inch heels and arched the small of her back in order to see the shot she wanted.

"Seven, side." The words were barely a breath of air as she took aim. As the ball spun toward its target she felt a little more of her tension ease and control reclaim its place in her body.

She'd simply forgotten his appeal over the past five months. Out of sight and all that. Which was proof enough that she had nothing to worry about. If she could so easily dismiss a man's sex appeal—and, oh, baby, did he ooze sex appeal—then he clearly wasn't a threat to her peace of mind.

By the time she'd lined up the ten ball, Tessa's nerves were as rock solid as her aim and her mind calm.

All she had to do was remember that she was in control. She didn't have to make changes at the magazine if she didn't want to. And as for Gabriel? Well, there wasn't a man alive who'd gotten the best of her. So why should this one be any different? Before her mind could begin a litany of warnings of why he was already different, she took aim and sent the cue ball sailing.

Just because he oozed the kind of charm that promised to leave her grateful when he broke her heart didn't mean she was going to let him. Silly man; he had no idea who he was dealing with. If he did, he'd know what every man had ever said about her since she'd turned fifteen was true—that Tessa Monroe's body might be hot as hell, but her heart was as cold as ice.

Ice, baby, she reminded herself with a chilly smile.

By the thirteen ball, she was comfortably confident again. Damned if she wouldn't enjoy putting Gabriel Thorne back in his place, she decided. She knew plenty of women who'd want a man like that at their feet, who'd want to make him into a pet just to prove they could. Not

Tessa. If she wanted something slobbering on her feet, she'd get a bulldog. Nope, the only place for a man like that was away from her. Far away.

Back in control, enjoying the inner peace that came with it, Tessa added a little hip wiggle to her next shot, letting her body zing with the delight as the balls cracked together.

"There's nothing prettier than a woman who's mastered the art of body English."

Damn it all to hell.

Tessa's heart jumped. She couldn't stop its silly reaction, but she made sure it didn't show. She didn't straighten. She didn't let her expression change. She simply lifted her gaze from the soothing expanse of green felt to the disturbing view on the other side of the pool table.

Dear lord, Gabriel Thorne took tall, dark and handsome to unbelievable lengths. From the broad expanse of well-muscled shoulders to the tips of his size-fourteen boots polished to a high gloss, he exuded strength. The sharp angles of his face, with its knife-edged cheekbones and golden skin, contrasted against hair so black it gleamed blue, and his eyes were just as dark.

Why did he have to be so freaking perfect?

Good-looking guys were a dime a dozen. Tessa was so jaded that sex appeal barely registered anymore. Power? It still inspired a little ping of sexual awareness in her belly but it was easy enough to ignore if she wanted.

But all three in a single man?

Almost irresistible.

Almost.

Gabriel Thorne, or Romeo as he was more suitably called, had one irredeemable strike against him.

He was actually Chief Petty Officer Gabriel Thorne.

US Navy SEAL.

Her stomach churned.

And the only thing higher on Tessa's off-limits list than a military man was a man so dedicated to the military that he devoted his life to becoming the best in order to serve in it.

"I came in here for a little privacy," she finally said, slowly straightening. As she did, she knew the draped neckline of her dress gaped, most likely offering a clear view all the way down to her skimpy pink panties. She reluctantly gave Gabriel credit when his eyes didn't shift from her face. Most men—no matter how well intentioned—couldn't resist a peek at the goods. "Why don't you be a doll and give it to me."

She waited for him to barge through that opening with a tasteless comment, actually hoping he would so she could find a solid, pinpointable reason to dislike him.

Because the excuse that he made her edgy wasn't working very well.

"C'mon, angel, don't you want to say hi after all these months?" he invited, his palms wide as if to invite her to c'mon over and do just that. Probably by wrapping her legs around his hips and planting a hot, juicy kiss on him. Or maybe that was just her little fantasy hello.

"That's the funny thing about distance. It doesn't always make the heart grow fonder," Tessa mused, leaning one hip on the pool table and swinging her foot. The move hitched her short skirt a little higher on her thigh, catching Romeo's eye. This, apparently, was on his approved list to ogle because his gaze heated as it skimmed over her smooth skin from the edge of her skirt to her hot pink toenails and right back up again.

"Now you're going to break my heart," he teased when his eyes met hers again. "Are you trying to say you didn't miss me?"

Despite his almost overwhelming appeal, Tessa was able to say quite honestly, "Nope, sorry. I didn't at all."

He gave her a long look, his eyes dark and almost spookily intense, as if he had some sort of power to see into people. Tessa lifted her chin, daring him to accept what he saw.

And waited, as her stomach clenched, to hear his opinion.

"I never took you for the type who hid at a party," he said instead, leaving Tessa to ignore the weird disappointment clenching her belly. "If I'd have had to guess, I'd figure you'd be front and center out there. A drink in hand, that gorgeous smile flashing as you flick off admirers and break hearts left and right."

"Isn't that an appealing visual?" Tessa mused, ignoring the reality of it. "Maybe I'll give it a try after I finish this round."

His eyes only left her for a moment, long enough to see that she only had two balls left. Instead of leaving, though, he leaned against the wall and gestured with his chin toward her hand.

"You seem to know your way around the stick."

Tessa made a show of sliding her fingers up the cue, skimming suggestively around the tip before sliding them right back down. Gabriel, being a man, watched the move and smiled. She just wished that smile wasn't so wickedly appealing. As much in defense against it as to replace the needy images flashing through her mind at the sight of him, she tapped the cue against her free hand a couple of times, then tilted the tip toward him in a mocking salute.

"Anytime you want me to take aim at your balls, you just give a whistle," she said, putting a little extrahusky suggestion in her tone. "You do know how to whistle, don't you?"

Gabriel's smile was pure appreciation, either for the movie quote or for her not-so-subtle threat. Knowing him, probably both.

"Angel, you want to play, I'm your man." He moved around the table so fast Tessa didn't have time to steel herself against the intense need that hit her when he reached her side. That was her excuse and she was sticking to it, dammit.

"I'll bet we'd have a fascinating game between us," he told her in that midnight voice of his. His fingers curled loosely over hers on the cue, guiding her hand back down toward the shaft. A zing of desire shot through Tessa's body, her knees shaking as heat, needy and intense, curled in her belly. Had she ever gone wet and weak with just a touch?

Only once, she admitted to herself as she tried to clear her head. Only once—the last time he'd touched her.

She stared at Romeo. His pitch-black eyes were bottomless. Not cold—just the opposite, in fact. They were so hot that Tessa was terrified she'd burn before she lost herself in those depths.

Since terror wasn't a feeling she was familiar with— or planned to experience long enough to get used to—she tilted her chin in challenge.

"Fascinating?" She put every bit of disinterest in her tone she could muster, keeping her expression amused. "Maybe. But it takes two to play, and I'm really not interested."

Arching a brow, she slid her hand out from under his and left him gripping the stick alone.

There.

She knew that comment would slay a lesser man. Send him falling to the floor with his hands over his assets— metaphorically speaking.

Gabriel wasn't a lesser man, but the refusal should still take care of him, she decided as she sashayed from the room.

A quick glance in the mirrored wall as she left gave her the perfect—and unobserved—look at his smile. Tessa tried not to groan.

Because that wicked grin said she'd been way too optimistic.

GABRIEL GAVE THE pool cue in his hand a light shake, absently checking the balance as he watched Tessa stride out, her hips swaying with enough temptation to send her skirt swirling around legs that had helped sell a million fitness videos.

The tiny purple dress was the same color as a breathtaking sunset he'd watched from a beach in Costa Rica a while back. Her long black hair tumbled in waves over her back and, despite the heels—damn, those had to be at least five inches—she was still as tiny as one of the Little People his Cherokee grandfather used to weave into stories around the campfire.

Shaking the memory away, Gabriel's easy smile faded into a frown. What was it was about Tessa Monroe that made him think of his past? Stupid, since he'd never met anyone like her before. Crazy, because the only place he had in his life for women was the present moment. And useless, since nobody knew better than Gabriel how important it was to defuse explosives before they blew up in his face. And there was nothing with more potential to detonate than the past.

And nothing more explosive than a sexy woman with an attitude.

"Yo, Romeo."

Gabriel blinked away his unusually deep thoughts and gave his buddy an easy smile.

"Yo, Scavenger," he drawled, watching the tall man move into the room with an air of someone escaping a torture chamber. "Had enough of the party already?"

"I'm not the one hiding in an empty room," Scavenger laughed, humor lighting his usually intense features. A first-class medic with recon skills that were nigh on magic as far as Gabriel was concerned, Scavenger tended to be on the quiet side. But he saw everything.

Something that Gabriel valued on the SEAL team.

But not in his private life.

Not that he had anything to hide. Hell, he was an open book. As long as the book opened to the page he was on today.

"What's up?" Gabriel asked, knowing that look in his friend's eyes. Part assessing, part caution, it meant the other guy was debating whether he wanted to share his thoughts or not.

"Jackrabbit's gonna be a pain in the ass," Scavenger finally said quietly, the words accompanied by a loose shrug.

Gabriel considered the warning. Because as casually as it was offered and as few words as it contained, if Scavenger had sought him out to say it, it was definitely a warning.

"There's always a period of adjustment when we join a new team," Gabriel pointed out, even though they'd been assigned to the team for six months already. Until they trained together, deployed together, they wouldn't feel like a team. "He'll get used to me."

"Don't think he'll get used to losing, though," Scavenger offered with a quick grin. "Watch your back. He's looking for an edge."

With a nod to acknowledge that he'd received the warning and would heed it—probably—Gabriel took aim at one of the last two balls on the table, letting it ricochet off the other to send both into different pockets.

"Thanks for missing the party out there to let me know," Gabriel said, meaning it. He might not care that some guy had issues, but he knew Scavenger's concern was the good of the team, which meant those issues would have to be dealt with. "You have to beat the women off with a stick yet?"

It was a source of never-ending amusement to Gabriel and most of the team that Scavenger, in all his shyness, was consistently hit on wherever they went.

"They wouldn't be all over me if you were there. Isn't that part of your rating? To take point on all social excursions, engage the female predators in order to allow the team to carry out their mission unmolested?"

"Is that what this is?" Gabriel laughed as he put the cue back in its stand. "You want me out there as a shield?"

"Nah, Irish was looking for you," Scavenger said, his cheeks a little toasty. "You were supposed to help him with something?"

Oh, yeah. He'd been on his way, then he'd gotten distracted by the vision of an angel. One look at Tessa Monroe's sweet little body curved over the pool table and his brain had straight-up fizzled. He'd been lucky he'd remembered his name when he'd stood across from her.

It was shaming for a man with his reputation to admit—even to himself—but if she'd crooked one of those sexy fingers of hers and led the way, he'd have followed her anywhere. Which meant she was dangerous. To his reputation, to his ego and to his peace of mind. All three of which Gabriel protected fiercely.

Gabriel had learned young to recognize trouble, a talent honed to perfection by his years in the military. But recognizing or not, he never ran from a fight, and he didn't back down from trouble.

But trouble like Tessa Monroe? An angel's face wrapped in a body that'd tempt the devil?

A wise man stepped carefully.

A wiser man plunged deep, reveled in the delight and found a way to walk away unscathed.

He just had to find his opening.

And he wasn't going to find it in here.

"I guess I'd better help Irish, and let you get back to the waiting ladies," Gabriel said.

The two men moved easily through the crowd toward the far side of the room, where it looked as if an entire platoon had gathered. Seeing the groom-to-be talking to an older woman who was the spitting image of Mitch's fiancée, Gabriel tapped Shane on the shoulder before tilting his head to indicate he was gonna do his duty.

"Chief Petty Officer Thorne, reporting for duty," Gabriel said when he reached Mitch and the woman who was apparently going to be his friend's mother-in-law.

Interest flashed in the blonde's eyes as she smiled. Mitch just shook his head in resigned amusement.

"Pauline, I'd like you to meet Gabriel Thorne. Gabriel, this is Livi's mother, Pauline." Waiting only long enough to finish the introductions, Mitch made his excuses to escape.

Leaving Gabriel alone with a cougar who looked as if she'd enjoy lapping him up for breakfast.

"Gabriel, thank you for your willingness to help make Mitchell and Olivia's wedding a beautifully memorable event. I've created a list for you," she said, unsnapping the tiny seashell-shaped purse dangling from her wrist to pull out a slip of paper. Gabriel was encouraged by its small size until she unfolded and unfolded and unfolded it again.

"That's quite a list," he observed, noting that the

computer-generated printout had multiple bullet points and appeared to be color coded.

"Read through it carefully, please, and let me know if there are any issues with the duties or timing." She handed it over with a smile that said she didn't care what he objected to.

"The ceremony will take place on Catalina Island in six weeks. Since it's a destination wedding, the events will span the entire first week of May. You'll need that entire week off. But if you could get time off beforehand to help with preparations, that would help, of course."

Gabriel squinted a little to see if she was joking. Seeing she wasn't, his lips twitched.

"Of course," he repeated, giving her the words she wanted to hear, but not the actual agreement. Because everyone knew how easygoing Uncle Sam was about letting entire SEAL teams go off the grid at the same time.

He glanced at the list, his eyes widening at the extent of duties listed. He'd executed complicated hostage rescue missions that hadn't required this many steps.

Then he gave those steps a closer look.

And saw how many of them had him paired with a certain angel-faced seductress. Gabriel's expression eased into a natural smile; that was to say, one that was filled with a whole lot of wicked.

Host beach bonfire, he noted.

Collaborate on romantic moonlight dance.

This could get interesting.

"Tessa Monroe is the—" he glanced at the top of the page, where it listed all of the players and their assigned roles "—maid of honor?"

"Mmm, yes. Tessa and Olivia have been friends for years, all the way back to college." When Gabriel gave her his most charming, do-tell-me-more smile, her own expression softened and she started chatting about Livi's time at San Diego State. Barracuda or not, the woman had good feelings for her kid. That brought her up a few notches in Gabriel's estimation. He knew firsthand that *mother* didn't mean *maternal*.

"When Livi launched her fitness videos, she brought Tessa in. I'm not sure Olivia could have achieved the level of success she did without her friend. Not only is Tessa a beautiful woman who has great camera presence, her being there made the touring and live events so much easier on Olivia."

"So Tessa's a trainer, too?" Gabriel asked, finally voicing one of the thousands of personal questions he hadn't let himself ask before.

"A trainer? Oh, no. Tessa doesn't have the patience to teach. She's actually a writer. Journalist?" Pauline frowned, then waved the distinction away as if it didn't matter. "She writes for a very successful digital magazine. I think she's also in charge of editorial, among other things. That enabled her to work from her laptop for weeks at a time while traveling. And, of course, her travels gave her so many new article ideas and contacts. I think two of the pieces she wrote on the road went on to win national attention."

Not sure why he felt so proud since it had nothing to do with him, Gabriel still smiled. Maybe because it proved what he'd already known. In addition to being gorgeous and sexy, Tessa was savvy and smart.

"It's a fitness magazine?"

"*Flirtatious*? No, it's more of a relationship magazine for singles. A lot of emphasis on sex, the mating games, bedroom games, how to use it all to get ahead." Pauline's voice dropped to a husky timbre as she reached out to trail her fingers along the back of his hand. "I'll be happy to share some of them, if you'd like?"

Gabriel blinked, surprised at how fast she went from businesslike to motherly to amused to cougar with barely a blink. Talented lady. But as attractive as she was, he didn't figure he'd be offering up more than his respect.

With that in mind, he lifted the list in a modified salute and suggested he find the groom and discuss the details.

"If you need anything, just call. My numbers are all there," Pauline instructed. Then she leaned forward and whispered a creative suggestion in his ear that made Gabriel's brows arch. Before he could refuse, she patted his ass and went on her way.

Amused, Gabriel headed in the opposite direction through the crowded ballroom. Figuring he'd earned it, he grabbed another beer on his way to where Mitch was seated.

"Did I offer my congratulations yet?" he asked, grabbing a chair, then straddling it before tilting his beer bottle toward his friend in a salute.

"So far you've offered three warnings, two enigmatic stares and the suggestion that I see a counselor," the groom-to-be mused with an easy smile. "You finally going to add a congrats to that?"

"On finding a sweetheart like Livi? Sure. But how about a word of advice?"

Mitch gestured with his own beer for Gabriel to go ahead.

"That was quite a chat with your future mother-in-law." Gabriel gave a silent whistle and shook his head. "You might wanna give thought to running."

"She's not so bad," Mitch responded, looking around. His gaze didn't land on the blonde barracuda who'd just propositioned Gabriel, but rested instead on her daughter.

"Not so bad?" Gabriel scoffed. "Did you get a load of my assignment list? I've served under admirals with less balls than she has."

Following Mitch's gaze, Gabriel glanced at his friend's fiancée. His eyes automatically shifted, though, to the dark-haired angel on the other side of the room, heat speeding through his system at the sight of her. A good-looking woman offering to ride him like a bronco got zip for reaction, but one look at Tessa and he was rock hard.

Damned if he could figure out what was going on.

He deliberately shifted his gaze away.

Lips twitching, he used his chin to indicate Mitch look that way, too.

"Your future mother-in-law has Scavenger in her sights."

Mitch followed his lead to where Pauline had the tall, quietly shy SEAL cornered. From the look of it, she was actually petting his chest.

"She'll eat him for breakfast," Mitch proclaimed, looking both amused and a little worried.

Over their friend's pending sexual education? Or the weirdness of watching all of the elements of his life mix together? Yet another reason to keep life to a single element, Gabriel figured.

"We should rescue him," Mitch said, starting to rise.

"Nah." Gabriel shook his head before Mitch could get to his feet. "It'll be good for him. A guy needs to push his comfort zone now and then."

"She might suck the comfort right out of him," Mitch muttered with a worried frown.

"Some women do that," Gabriel mused, his gaze cutting across the room to lock on Tessa again.

She was so damned sexy, her smile wide and bright in a way it never was when she looked at him.

Time to change the game, he decided.

He'd played it with amused distance already, and all that'd done was let her get a hold somewhere in the back of his mind.

As he listened with half an ear to Mitch talking, he realized that since Tessa was like no woman he'd ever known before, he'd have to take a different approach in dealing with her.

He was simply going to have to pursue her. That he'd have her went without question, since it was obviously the only way he'd get her out of his system.

He was a man who knew how to strategize, how to plan and how to win.

And he never, ever gave up.

Since Tessa wasn't on board with his plan, he'd see her as a mission.

A target to be assessed, evaluated and overcome.

He'd figure her out.

He'd have her—on his terms.

Then he'd do what he always did.

Walk away, leaving both of them satisfied.

3

TESSA DIDN'T CHECK to see if Gabriel was looking her way. She didn't have to. She knew his eyes were locked on her. She felt the heat of his interest all the way to her belly, where desire curled, unwanted, in a tightly coiled fire just waiting to explode.

Ignoring the edgy call of desire, she smiled and dished out friendly greetings and easy small talk as she worked the room. This was what she did. Socialized, flitted and fluttered, leaving a trail of lust and smiles behind. And if she did it with a little stress still weighing her down, well, hey, nobody else had to know that.

Not that anyone would. Nobody ever looked deep enough to see more than the outer package anyway.

Except Livi.

Still, Tessa gave it her best shot by amping up her smile and focusing on keeping her body at ease as she slid into the chair next to her best friend.

"Hey, you," Livi greeted. "I was starting to wonder where you were. Pauline was talking about sending out a search party but I convinced her to wait until appetizers."

"Thanks for saving me that." Tessa pulled a face at the idea of Livi's über–control freak of a mother coming in search of her. She wasn't sure if that would have been better or worse than Romeo.

"Champagne?" a waiter offered.

After a quick glance at the glass, Tessa gestured to Livi's flute of sparkling cider.

"I'll have what she's having," she decided, giving him a warm smile that almost made him fumble the tray.

"What's wrong?" Livi asked, her brows drawing together.

"Wrong? Why is it wrong that I'm keeping my pregnant friend company in her drinking choices?" Tessa said with a shrug.

That sounded much better than admitting that she couldn't quite bring herself to celebrate what she was sure was going to be a painful mistake on Livi's part. Marriage itself was bad enough. But marriage because she was pregnant? To a military guy?

"Since when do you drink the same thing I do? You're upset. I can tell," Livi said with a worried frown. Then her gaze slid past Tessa, the striking blonde's eyes sharpening a little. Tessa didn't need to turn around to know that her friend had just spotted the reason for her irritation.

"Are you and Gabriel at it again?" Livi asked, her frown deepening as she shook her head. "I don't get it. I've never seen anyone argue with Gabriel except you."

"But he's so easy to argue with," Tessa intoned. At Livi's impatient look, she gave a dismissive wave of her hand. "I wasn't arguing with him. Really. An issue blew up at the magazine this afternoon that has me a little edgy is all."

Not all a lie, Tessa mentally defended, since she hadn't actually argued with Gabriel. A covert threat to whack him with the pool cue didn't an argument make. And she *had* ended her workday with drama.

Usually, *Flirtatious* was a source of pleasure for Tessa. The magazine she'd founded with Jared Welch and Maeve Bannion was a huge success not only for her ego, but for her bank account.

But like sexy men, even a great career had its irritating moments.

"What did Jared do?" Livi asked, correctly honing in on one of the sources of Tessa's troubles. "You need to watch out, Tessa. I know you think you've got a handle on him, but he's a snake."

"Please." Tessa laughed. She wasn't worried about Jared. Between her and Maeve, they kept him in line. Mostly. "When has a man ever got the better of me?"

She deliberately kept her gaze locked on Livi instead of searching the room for Romeo. Talk about ruining her reputation. She didn't want anyone thinking she was nervous over a guy, even a guy like him.

"Jared would like nothing more than to ride on the tails of your success until he found a way to shove you out of the equation," Livi said slowly, her eyes locked on Tessa's face. "You've been getting more and more attention, syndication of your articles is picking up and you've had some amazing interviews."

All true. Tessa was one hell of a writer. Oh, she knew Jared liked to tout her as a journalist, but she had no illusions. She wrote very fun, sassy and sexy pieces that all centered around the games between women and men. Flirtations, as the magazine's name suggested. One Hundred and One Ways to Flirt Your Way to Success, Top Five Pick-up Lines for Savvy Women and The ABCs of Mastering the Sexual Playground were just a few of her recent submissions. Hardly Pulitzer-worthy topics, but they suited her talents and personality, they were extremely popular and they were fun to write. All key reasons why she loved her job.

Jared wouldn't mess that up. Would he?

Tessa rubbed a finger against the throbbing in her temple, wondering when men had shifted from being a delightful pastime to being a pain in her butt.

"I'm filming a yoga segment tomorrow," Livi said. "Why don't you join in? A little balance, a little positive energy, it'd be good for you. I could use a toned body in belly-baring workout gear to bump the ratings."

Tessa considered it for a moment. A nationally renowned fitness celebrity with a string of successful videos, Livi had just secured a contract with a fitness cable channel to air her new live workout program that she'd titled *Stages*, for women at every stage of life.

If there was a frustrated, irritated and inappropriately horny stage, Tessa was the girl to represent it. She was also the woman who knew better than to give in to that particular cocktail of emotions since it only led to trouble.

"You're focusing on pregnancy workouts right now, aren't you?" Tessa remarked with a laugh. "I'm not sure breathing positive energy to my uterus is going to relax me a whole lot."

"I'm the only pregnant woman in the crew," Livi countered with a wave of her hand. "There's a new mom, a retired nurse, a teen and an older man, too. That's the point of these workouts. They work for everyone. But if you don't want to work out, why don't we do a spa day? Massage, facial, mani-pedi. The works."

"It sounds great, but I should probably go into the office. I'll chat with Maeve, see if she's got any idea what's going on," she said.

"Work over pampering," Livi said, pretending to be shocked. "That doesn't sound like the Tessa Monroe I know."

Tessa grimaced. It didn't, did it?

A rare and unwelcome feeling of uncertainty washed

over her. Was it her life that was in turmoil? Or was it her that didn't fit her once-perfect lifestyle?

The worry that'd been following her around like an itchy backpack took on yet another layer. Tessa leaned in to ask Livi's advice. Before she could say a word, though, she felt a chill over her shoulder.

"What's this I hear?" Pauline said as she slid into a seat next to them. "Our wild child is losing her edge?"

Tessa's urge to confess disappeared.

If she'd learned one lesson good and well at her momma's knee, it was to never show weakness. Especially not to a woman like Pauline. Or the blonde barracuda, as Livi's video crew called her.

With just a twitch of her chin, Tessa's confidence was back. Her smile turned sharp, her body language sliding into sassy as she turned to greet Livi's mom.

"I'm as edgy as can be," she claimed, lifting her glass of sparkling cider to toast the older woman. "How about you, Pauline? Now that Livi's off the market, are you going to hit the clubs with me?"

"You won't have time for clubbing," Pauline said, waving the invitation away with the same lack of enthusiasm as it was offered. "The wedding is going to take a great deal of time and energy. As maid of honor, a lot of the work is going to fall to you. I hope you're capable of handling it, Tessa. I'd hate to see Olivia having to pick up the slack if you're out playing games. Or worse, to have her dream wedding turn into a disappointment."

"Mother," Livi growled, her sweet face turning ferocious.

As much fun as it would be to see her friend stand up to the woman who until a couple of months ago had run her life, Tessa knew the stress wasn't good for Livi, or for the baby.

She laid her hand over Livi's clenched fist and gave it a squeeze before angling her body just a little. Enough to put herself between daughter and mother.

"Please," she told Pauline with a dismissive laugh. "When have I *ever* left anyone disappointed? I'll do everything in my power to give Livi the wedding of a lifetime."

After another few seconds with that assessing stare, Pauline gave a slow nod.

What the hell? Tessa wanted to ask. Since when did she merit doubt?

A tight, aching ball of doubt knotted in her stomach, all of her worries from the evening feeding the pain.

Was Pauline inadvertently right? Was she losing her edge?

A couple stopped at the table to congratulate Livi. As the bride-to-be and Pauline fell into conversation with them, Tessa's worried gaze wandered the room.

When her eyes landed on the sexiest man she'd ever known, the only man who might possibly be more than she could handle, her frown deepened. Instead of backing up Gabriel Thorne against that poolroom wall, stripping him naked and riding him like a bucking bronco, she'd run away. Why? Was she afraid she couldn't handle him?

Tessa exchanged her cider for champagne and took a contemplative sip. Wetting her lips and letting the taste of the sweet bubbles coat her tongue, she shoved aside her earlier fears. Being worried about not handling any man— even a man like Gabriel Thorne—was about as crazy as being afraid of having body-melting, pleasure-screaming multiple orgasms. Something she was quite sure he could provide, with a few interesting twists thrown in.

A shot of lust speared straight through her, landing low in her belly with a familiar sexual zing.

That was the perfect answer, she realized.

She was going to seduce Romeo.

Not only would it get him out of her system, but it would also prove that she was just as edgy and in control as ever.

And then, emotionally steady, mentally refreshed and physically sated, she could do what she always did with men.

Thank him for the good time, consign him to her been-there-done-that list and, more important, move on with making her life exactly what she wanted it to be.

Fun and easy.

WELL, WELL.

Gabriel wasn't sure what'd changed.

Maybe it was a couple of glasses of wine.

Maybe the sun had fully set.

Hell, maybe it was the spices on the grilled-prawn appetizers circulating around the room.

Whatever it was, Tessa had gone from icily pretending he didn't exist to giving him assessing looks that were hot enough to melt his shorts from twenty yards away.

She hadn't approached, nor had she done more than look. But a woman like Tessa? She knew how to say one hell of a lot with just a glance.

He kinda liked it.

He just wasn't sure what he wanted to do about it yet.

Oh, sure, his melting shorts and their happy contents knew exactly what they'd like to do.

But a man didn't live through countless missions, a war and a childhood that put both to shame without learning to carefully question a gift horse before sticking anything in its mouth. Even if the gift horse was the sexiest filly he'd ever seen.

Her big blue eyes were even more appealing filled with sexual speculation. Not to dis the chilly disdain from before. That'd been kinda sexy, too.

"You ever notice how parties like this tend to have rumors flowing right along with the booze?"

Gabriel tipped back his beer bottle for a drink before slanting Jackrabbit a sideways look. He didn't say anything, though, figuring the guy could bait his own hook for this little fishing trip.

"Rumors like the one that says that your success with the ladies is nigh on legendary," the other man continued in a musing tone. "Can you believe it? Legendary."

"Well, you know what they say about rumors, don't you?" Seeing where this was going, Gabriel's grin was as sharp as his tone was casual. "They're like smoke."

Jackrabbit pulled a face before nodding. "And where there's smoke, there's fire."

"I like serving with a guy who thinks fast."

"I heard a lot of other rumors tonight. Wonder how hot they are."

"You looking to start your own gossip site specializing in Navy news?"

"Nah, just getting to know the guys I'll be serving with. It pays to have a good handle on the team's successes, right? And on their failures."

"You keep digging around in those rumors, you'll hear one sure truth." Gabriel's smile turned deadly. "I don't fail."

"Then you won't mind a little bet based on one of the rumors I heard?"

His instincts said to tell the guy to get a different hobby.

But Gabriel's entire world revolved around his service to the SEALs. Which meant he put his team ahead of everything. So making peace with this idiot for the good of morale before they went into training was the right thing to do.

"What's the bet?"

"I heard that for all your legendary prowess with

women, you've been shot down in flames by one particular lady. Tessa Monroe, who, if I hear right, is as wild as she is sexy." Jeglinski's smile turned mean. "That had to bite, being turned down by a woman like that. Even worse to have her blowing you off like I saw earlier. Damn, man, those were some cold looks she was sending your way."

Not bothering to wonder who had spread that bit of news, or resent that it was true, Gabriel focused instead on keeping his expression amused as he waited for the rest.

"So here's the wager. I'll bet you can't get the sexy Tessa Monroe into bed. Given that we're gonna be busy for the next few months training in the Pacific, I'll even give you until Irish says 'I do.'"

So pissed he actually saw little red spots dancing through his vision, Gabriel had to call up every bit of control to keep from grabbing the guy by the throat. He wanted to pound the guy so hard they'd have to change his call sign to Flatrabbit. Who the hell was this idiot, objectifying women that way? Talking about Tessa as if she was a piece of tail or trampy frog hog who chased SEALs for sex.

"Bro, you might want to do a little studying. One of the reasons for my legendary success with the ladies is probably beyond your comprehension, but it's rather simple." Gabriel stepped forward, getting into the other man's space with a chilly smile made all the colder by his icy tone. "It's called respect. I never offer them anything less."

"Does that mean you're backing down?"

Disgusted, Gabriel turned on his heel and strode away without bothering to answer.

A quarter hour later, he stood on the beach at the base of the mansion's steps, hands shoved in his pockets as the sight of the ocean soothed away his anger.

He'd learned young the dangers of losing control.

Whether it was because of anger or alcohol, the damage was the same.

Jackrabbit was an ass, but Gabriel recognized his type. A small dog protecting its territory did the same thing. Yapped challenges it couldn't meet, trying to look tough. He'd back down once he'd accepted the new order of things. And now that Gabriel and Scavenger were assigned to Coronado permanently along with Irish, that new order could begin.

"Look at you, out here all by your lonesome."

The ocean washed over the words, the evening air trying to carry them away. But it didn't take his SEAL training to recognize a female voice.

His mouth almost dropped open when he saw who it was.

"Tessa?"

"Hey there," she said with a smile that sparkled with more than just a greeting. "It's so pretty out here. Much nicer than all that stuffy air in there."

Tessa tilted her head toward the manor, but her eyes didn't leave his face as she descended the last few steps to join him in the sand. As soon as she did, her feet sank and she grabbed hold of his arm as if she were keeping her balance.

"Mmm, you are in peak condition, aren't you?" she said as her hand wrapped around his biceps and squeezed. "I don't think there's a bigger turn-on than a man with a rock-hard body. And you are quite…hard."

She let the last word drop off her lips on a sigh, her expression appreciatively seductive.

Gabriel frowned.

What the hell was she doing?

"Is everything okay?" he asked.

Still holding on to him, she bent one slender leg to slide

off her shoe, then, the sky-high heel dangling from a strap, she shifted hands to remove the other one.

Gabriel watched the moonlight skim over her bare legs, whimsically wondering if she'd turn into a mermaid if she got too close to the water. Or, more likely, into a siren.

"Everything is just fine," she said once she'd carefully set her shoes, one upright next to the other, on the bottom step.

This was the first time he'd seen her barefoot. A wave of protectiveness washed over him when he realized how tiny she actually was. Her personality was so big, her sexuality so intense, that it was easy to overlook her size.

Then she smiled, her lips curved and enticing, her eyes glinting with sultry amusement as she speared her fingers into her hair, lifting the dark curls before letting them fall to her shoulders again. Her pleasure at such a simple, yet sensual act sent a shaft of heat straight to Gabriel's dick.

With any other woman he'd figure this was an invitation.

But Tessa wasn't any woman.

"So what's the deal? You were bored in there?" he mused randomly.

"Actually, I'm here to see if you wanted to play," she said in a sexy tone. She slid her hand over his arm again, the brush of her fingers echoing her words' husky caress.

"Play?" he repeated, his eyes narrowed.

"Play," she confirmed with a teasing smile.

Sure she was.

And he was the one being played.

Even if the board was being run by a master he could still see the signs.

And Tessa Monroe was most definitely a master. At games of all kinds. And at running.

He debated calling her out on the move. But the deliberation only lasted a moment before he acknowledged that the risk was high and the payoff low. If he pointed out that he could see the game, she'd probably skip out again. It was probably what she was expecting.

As he stared down into her face, so delicate, yet so vivid, he realized that he was starting to understand her.

Gabriel knew the minute Tessa could pigeonhole him, she'd dismiss him. That was what she did with men. He understood her, since in many ways she was his own mirror image.

Just sexier.

She was also wickedly protective of her friends, appeared to value nothing more than loyalty and had a sweet streak he was sure she'd deny. And since despite her obvious misgivings, she'd agreed to be Livi's maid of honor, she clearly put her friends' feelings over her own.

The woman was a study in contrasts and spelled trouble for any man looking for peace and tranquility.

Good thing for him he wanted neither.

"So?" Tessa said, wetting her bottom lip with her tongue and sending a shaft of passion spiking through his system. "What do you say? Want to play?"

He leaned back on his heels, considering her face. It was a study in seduction. The full, pouting lips, the sweep of her lashes. But he could see the calculation in the blue depths of her eyes, there beneath the desire.

And in a flash as powerful as his spiking desire, he realized what she was doing.

She wanted to fan this heat, accelerate it so it blew hot, fast and furious. She figured the faster it blew up, the quicker it blew out, the sooner it'd be over. Then she'd turn on those sexy heels of hers and walk away without a glance.

Without giving him another thought.

Gabriel totally understood her strategy. He even admired it.

But he'd be damned if he was going to make it easy for her.

He didn't know why.

It was stupid to worry about dragging out this thing between them. It was obviously hot enough to set off fire alarms already. Could it really get any hotter? Any wilder?

And then there was his personal policy to live for the moment. Today was the only day he was guaranteed to have, so today was to be lived to the fullest.

But whatever this was between them, and he had no idea what it might be, Gabriel was damned if it was going to be finished until he was ready.

It might take weeks.

Maybe months.

He might be finished after one orgasm or it could be dozens.

But hey, it didn't matter if it was on the battlefield, behind covert cover or between the sheets.

He was a man used to giving his all.

And when it was done, she might walk away.

But she'd never forget him.

He'd make damned sure of that.

It was time to put Operation Romance into play.

With that in mind, Gabriel took Tessa's hand, and in a move he'd never made before but felt completely natural, he lifted it to his lips.

"What are you doing?"

Underneath the surprise, he heard the nerves dancing there, just beneath the surface. And he reveled in them.

He'd thrown her off.

Which was a great first step.

"Doing? I'm seducing you," he said quietly, taking his

time as he slid his hands through the long sweep of her hair, enjoying the silky thickness weighing against his fingers. "Since you've finally admitted this attraction we've got going on here, I figure it's time to see how far we can push it. How long we can play it out."

"Oh, I'll bet you're good for at least a few long, hard hours," she said in a husky tone, her fingers tiptoeing up his chest, leaving hot little trails wherever they touched.

"Oh, yeah, I could keep you panting and wet for hours and hours," he promised, leaning closer as if to kiss her. At the last second, he shifted so his lips brushed the softest whisper over her silken cheek. "But I was thinking we could do better than that."

Her breath hitched a little; her eyes blurred with pleasure. Her fingers were kneading his chest, nails digging in gently in a sexy rhythm that promised a superb sense of timing.

For a second, Gabriel wanted to say to hell with dragging this out. It wasn't ego reminding him that he'd never had a woman who didn't want more when they were done. The simple truth was that he was damned good at sex.

The problem was, so was Tessa. He was sure of it. And she was a woman with exquisite control. He had no doubt that while she might, if forced, admit as she left his bed that it'd been the best sex of her life, she'd still leave.

He had to hook her good and solid first, so she'd be there until he'd had his fill.

"See, real seduction is an art," he continued, making it up as he spoke. "There's a smooth buildup, layers of needs and awareness. There's discovery, finding out if we have the same turn-ons, exploring each other's secret delights."

Her eyes sharpened to a blue so deep it was almost purple, those full lips parted just a little as if ready for him to dive in. Damn, she was intoxicating.

He was halfway there, his mouth craving the taste of hers, before he yanked himself back.

To hide his slip, he rubbed his thumb over the soft cushion of her bottom lip instead.

"All of that should come first, don't you think?" he said with his most charming smile.

Watching the play of emotions flash through Tessa's eyes, excitement melding with fear, worry with passion, he gave himself a mental pat on the back.

Damned if this wasn't going to beat the hell out of fast and furious.

Figuring he deserved a little reward for outmaneuvering her, Gabriel pulled Tessa closer. Pleasure pounded through him as the delicious curves of her body aligned tightly against his hard planes.

He knew his limits, knew exactly how far he could push this desire before he hit the point of no return.

Now to find out hers.

4

HER BODY WAS on fire.

Hot, molten pleasure radiated out from every point it came into contact with the deliciously hard planes of Romeo's body. He towered over her, his eyes as dark as the sky above as he stared down at her. His fingers were a whisper as they skimmed over her cheek before sliding into her hair, rubbing a strand between them before tucking it behind her ear.

With a focus that held incredible promise for things to come, he leaned closer.

Tessa's heart clenched, anticipation coiling tight around desire as she waited to see what he would do. She'd been secretly dreaming about his lips for months. Wondering what they'd feel like. Would he be forceful and take her mouth? Or would he gently seduce?

Their eyes locked on each other's, Gabriel's smile flashed for just a second. The closer he came, the more excited she got. At the last second, before he reached her lips, he changed direction. Tessa shivered as his breath whispered over her ear a heartbeat before his lips.

Oh. As his mouth brushed her flesh, anticipation uncoiled, sending that desire shooting through her system.

Holy screaming orgasms.

With one hand pressed to the small of her back and the other curled into her hair and just the sweetest brush of his mouth, Romeo sent her from intrigued and cautious to wet and needy. She sank her fingers into his biceps, delighting in the sensations.

Tessa was a woman exquisitely in tune with her own body, brilliantly aware of the nuances that played out between women and men and fiercely sensitive to the potentially emotional missteps.

Which, she remembered as a knot of panic balled in her belly, at odds with the feeling of throbbing desire, was why she'd determined so many months ago that Romeo was off-limits.

Because he was dangerous on so very many levels.

She gave an involuntary hum as his teeth nipped at her earlobe, the sharp pleasure shooting through her body like a wake-up message to her erogenous zones.

Tessa was also a woman of fierce pride.

She'd come out here to seduce Romeo for a very good reason.

And just because it was a mistake—probably a huge mistake—didn't mean those reasons weren't still valid.

She pressed her palms against the rock-solid walls of his chest, her fingers kneading before she skimmed them down to his waist and around to cup his sexy butt. The move pulled his body closer to hers. Since she was barefoot and he was at least six foot tall, the evidence of just how huge he was pressed temptingly against her stomach.

Oh, yeah, baby.

What better way to prove her power than to take on something so huge, so big, so overpowering—Tessa's thighs trembled as images, mostly naked, flashed through her head.

As if he were reading her mind and had decided to reward her for coming to the very decision he wanted, Gabriel's mouth slid over her cheek again. Whispering kisses trailed from her ear to the corner of her mouth.

She parted her lips, keeping the invitation subtle. But smart guy that he was, Romeo grabbed the invite and ran with it. Whisper soft, he rubbed his lips over hers. His kiss was as gentle as the breeze dancing around them and just as innocuous. She breathed in his scent, fresh like the ocean beyond, and Tessa's heart sighed at the sweetness of his kiss. Her mind was a little amused that she'd gotten all worked up and worried over something this, well, nice. But hey, better to overreact than underestimate.

Who said sexual chemistry led to explosions? She laughed in the back of her head. Not minding that this was one of the few times she'd misread sexual potential, she skimmed her hands from his arms to his shoulders, then comfortably linked her fingers behind his neck. Relaxed and ready to enjoy the warmth, she loosened her guard and leaned a little closer.

Later, she'd wonder if Romeo had some sort of triggering device that told him when her defenses had hit their lowest. Because that was when he made his move.

Romeo's hands shifted from her hair to cup her butt, pulling her tight against his body. His mouth angled, lips widening as he shifted gears from sweet to sexy with the slip of his tongue.

Before she could do more than gasp, he plunged.

His teeth scraped over her bottom lip, his tongue sweeping her mouth, luring hers into his before tangling them together so tight, so close, that her brain didn't even have time to send up warning signals.

It was too busy exploding.

Right along with her body.

Tessa felt as if she were melting, floating on a sea of sensations.

As Romeo's mouth moved over hers, her entire being leaned into the kiss.

Amazing.

Deliciously, mind-bogglingly, warning-signal-worthy amazing.

Every single portion of her being was focused on him.

On his mouth as it slid over hers.

On the taste of him coating her tongue, rich and addicting.

On the feel of his hands, rough and demanding on her hips.

On the intensity of his body as it pressed tight against her soft curves.

Mmm, he was delicious.

Her fingers skimmed over the soft cotton of his dress shirt, over the hard breadth of his shoulders, delighting in the powerful muscles there. She scraped her nails down his chest, giving a low purr deep in her throat at his body's instant reaction. His hips thrust, his hands tightened on her hips and his tongue stabbed deeper into her mouth, demanding even more.

She hummed low in her throat like a satisfied cat, reveling in the pleasure of their passion.

She'd known it'd be like this.

That he'd feel like the answer to her every sexual fantasy.

That he'd know just where to touch, just how to move, to make her ready to beg for more.

Tessa's head fell back, inviting Gabriel to have more.

His lips skimmed over her flesh, soft as air until he unerringly found the spot there, just beneath her ear, just above her shoulder. He scraped it with his teeth, tongue sliding hot and molten over her flesh.

Tiny tremors rocked through her body, her panties damp with passion as Tessa pressed her thighs together tightly to intensify the feeling.

If he could do this with just a simple brush of his lips, with his hands in neutral and his shaft still zipped away, what would he do when they got naked and crazy?

Her mind boggled at the possibilities.

She shivered with excitement, her body demanding more, begging for fulfillment.

And her stomach—always the harbinger of stress to come—clenched tight enough to be felt over the excitement there.

Tessa usually reveled in her passions and was on intimate terms with her desires.

It wasn't the passion that scared her.

It was the need.

Edgy, intense and demanding.

She wanted to believe she'd have been able to resist it if she hadn't been lulled into complacency with that sweet starter of a kiss. But she knew better. The way her body was trembling, dancing on the edge of a fully clothed, erogenous-zone-free orgasm, was a sure sign that she was in big time trouble if she didn't grab control back.

Fast.

It took everything she had, but Tessa was finally able to pull away from Romeo's mouth. Stepping back, she almost lost her balance in the sand. Planting her feet, she pretended that was the only place she was teetering and took a deep breath.

Even with the much-needed distance between her and Romeo, she could still feel him.

His hands, hot and enticing on her body.

His lips, wild and demanding on her mouth.

His erection, hard and throbbing against her thigh.

Without thinking, Tessa's gaze dropped to the front of his slacks, her smile taking a wicked slant at the evidence there. Of his desire for her, yes. But also of how incredibly, deliciously, temptingly huge he was.

And just like that, lust overcame fear and Tessa was ready to put that huge temptation to good use.

"I'd say you've got a pretty solid handle on the art of seduction," she said with a teasing smile, closing the distance between them again.

His eyes were hooded, but she could see the desire in their depths. And something else. Tessa didn't look too close, telling herself she didn't want that sort of intimacy. This was all about physical satisfaction. She didn't want to know what was going on behind his gorgeous face. Feelings, thoughts, emotions—those would just get in her way.

"And you're pure temptation," he said quietly, his hands resting on her hips again. Her smile widened as she felt the restraint in them. How long would it take her to break that control of his? She'd bet anything she could snap it before she lost hers. Her smile widening at the private challenge, she prepared to win.

"*This* is definitely tempting," she whispered, pressing kisses to his chest. She didn't even remember unbuttoning his shirt, but she knew his hands had been occupied so it must have been her. "Tempting enough that I definitely want to see more. But I suppose getting naked on the beach isn't the best idea."

She watched through her lashes, waiting for him to take the invitation, wondering where he'd go with it. A five-star hotel or the backseat of his car? Both had their own appeal.

"Where do you like to get naked?" he asked instead, his eyes hot on her face with an intimate knowledge. As if he not only already knew where and how she liked to get naked, but also exactly what she looked like.

Tessa shivered as anticipation sent delighted tingles through her body.

"Wherever it feels good." Not that she got naked every time it felt good, or in every place presented to her. But she knew that her reputation as a sex kitten was as appealing to most men as her toned body or her pretty face. So she rarely disabused them of the idea that she'd done anything and everyone.

"Do you like candlelight?" he asked softly, his fingers skimming a light pattern over her bare shoulder and down the draping bodice of her dress.

Tessa's breath caught as he traced gently over the lush mounds of her breasts where they spilled out of the silk. Her nipples peaked, aching and stiff, inviting him to slide beneath the fabric and say hello.

"There is a lot of appeal in candlelight," she murmured, barely aware of her words because every ounce of her focus was on those fingers.

Skimming closer and closer. With one deep breath she could lift her nipples to meet those fingers. But the anticipation, the game of waiting, was too exciting to end so soon.

"Wine?"

"Mmm, intoxicating," she breathed, although she knew no amount of alcohol could touch the heady delight he was stirring in her body.

"Music?"

The sound of the pounding surf and whistling wind were enough for her, but she'd feel gauche saying something that clichéd.

Then something clicked in the back of her head. Tessa forced her heavy eyelids up so she could peer at him. With his face still buried in the curve of her neck and his mouth doing wild things to her pulse, all she could see was the top of his head. She frowned a little as she tried to see where his questions were leading.

"I'm already tempted enough to want a taste of you, Romeo," she purred. "I don't need clichéd trappings and flirtatious fluff."

"Trappings?" he said, his breath a warm puff of air over her shoulder, making her shiver as he laughed. Lifting his head, Romeo gave her an amused look, the mirth in his eyes putting her back up for some reason.

"Angel, romance isn't about trappings. It's about style."

"Romance?" Ice poured through her, instantly chilling the passion. "Why ruin a good time with silly ideas like that?"

"Some women find romance appealing," he pointed out.

Tessa blinked. What was going on? She was talking about getting naked and he wanted to bounce around the merits of emotional platitudes?

"Some women don't believe in romance," Tessa said with a stiff laugh. "Starry-eyed teens and eternal optimists might think it's real. But c'mon, we know better."

His smile didn't shift. If anything, he looked even more satisfied at her words than put off.

"You don't believe in romance?" he asked.

"Not even a little bit." Impatience at war with confusion, both overlaid by a healthy coating of lust, Tessa gently scraped her nails over his gorgeously impressive chest and arched one brow. "But I do believe in satisfaction. So why don't we give that a try?"

HAD HE EVER been more tempted in his life?

Gabriel was pretty sure that answer was a big fat no.

"Here's the thing." Despite his body's protests, Gabriel focused on the bigger picture and reluctantly peeled one of Tessa's hands off his chest. He brushed his lips over her knuckles before giving her a sexy wink. "I'll bet we can have even more satisfaction with a little extra effort."

"I'll bet we could," she said with a look hot enough to melt the zipper of his slacks. She shifted her hand to rub her thumb over his lower lip, running the tip of her tongue over her own at the same time.

Gabriel groaned. He'd engaged in some imaginative foreplay over the years, but he was pretty sure this was the first time he'd played a game that kept him entertained, intrigued and turned on all at the same time.

Unable to resist, he leaned down to mimic her move, running his own tongue over her mouth. It was like sipping ambrosia, the taste of her filling his senses with the promise of ecstasy.

"Let's go," she suggested breathlessly, her lips soft against his as her hands skimmed down his chest once again, leaving trails of fire in their wake.

"Go where?" Gabriel teased, knowing damned well where she wanted to go. To ecstasy's gate, a place he was very familiar with, having spent a great deal of time there. He had a feeling that visiting there with Tessa would be beyond anything he'd ever known before.

He could show her a damned good time.

Make her scream with pleasure, whimper with need.

He'd be the best she ever had. He was sure of it.

He wanted to.

Damned if he didn't.

But he had a plan. A mission.

And a man never walked away from his mission until it was complete.

Still, it took all of his willpower to ease back on the kiss. Like a man about to go on a weeklong fast, he drew in the taste of Tessa as if he could live off her flavor until he got his mouth on her again.

He'd made a living out of tempting fate, doing the

impossible. He was trained to take risks and prevent explosions.

But pulling away from Tessa was just about the hardest thing Gabriel had ever done.

Like working with any volatile situation, he eased back slowly. He kept his expression neutral, friendly even. His eyes watchful, senses on full alert, he took a careful breath to settle his pulse. Another to ensure he was focused and steady.

Then, and only then, he offered her a charming smile.

"You're amazing," he said truthfully. "But we can't have sex tonight."

Tessa's lush lashes fluttered as she blinked, her sharply arched brows drawing together before she shook her head as if clearing her ears.

"I'm sorry?" she said as she looked askance.

Gabriel barely managed to keep from laughing aloud at the expression on her face.

God, he loved confusing her.

Not quite as much as he enjoyed pleasuring her, of course. But enough that it was easy to shift from one to the other if it'd guarantee an extension of the pleasure until he was ready.

"I said—"

"Is this some sort of SEAL superstition?" she asked, peering at him through narrowed eyes. "Like if you step on a crack you'll break your partner's back? Or that if you change your socks before a mission you'll endanger the entire team?"

His lips twitched. He was pretty sure that not changing his socks would be more danger to the team.

"Because if it's a matter of endangering one of your missions—or at least, endangering it in your mind—I totally understand."

At his surprised look, Tessa shrugged. "Hey, I can be patriotic. Call it my way of supporting our troops...or in this case, you."

If she'd whipped an AK-47 out from beneath her tiny little dress and knocked him upside the head with it, Gabriel couldn't have been more floored. Had anyone outside of the team itself ever been so unquestionably supportive of what he did? His mind was blank, so he took that as a no.

"You're so damned sweet," he said, frowning a little. Sweet, patriotic, sexy and funny. Something in his chest tightened as he stared at the beauty that was Tessa's face and realized that he'd barely scratched the surface of this gorgeous woman. And now, more than anything, he was determined to delve deep until he'd learned every single thing about her that he could.

He didn't know what that feeling was going on in his gut right now since he'd never felt anything like it before. But it demanded to be acknowledged. So he did just that in the only way he knew how.

He kissed her again. But before it could get too hot, even heavier, he made himself stop. Slowly, reluctantly, he pulled back with a heavy sigh.

"I want to take you out," he said after clearing his throat. "Dinner, dancing, maybe a moonlight walk on the beach."

"Out?"

"A date."

"Mmm," she breathed as she leaned closer again. Her tongue slid along his bottom lip before she gave it a gentle nip. "Why don't we skip to another type of moonlight dance? A naked one that includes a myriad of hip thrusts and slow grinds."

"Because as much as I really, really want to get naked together and worship each other's bodies, I want to romance you first. I'm going to show you what it feels like to build the anticipation and layer the needs," he promised. "You're going to want me so badly by the time I'm through that all it'll take is a touch to send you flying over the edge of screaming pleasure."

"And you're going to make me wait for this? Not for the good of your team or because you're superstitious?"

"Yep. Because I'm going to romance you first."

Tessa was looking at him as if he'd lost his mind.

All things considered, Gabriel wasn't so sure that he hadn't.

Especially when he watched her turn from hot to cold with just a sweep of those lashes.

"Let me get this straight," she said, stepping back to give him a chilly look. "You are turning me down? Walking away from your only shot because you want, what was it? Romance?"

Well, when she put it that way, he sounded like an idiot. Unable to stop himself, Gabriel frowned. He was pretty sure he'd never had anyone question his intelligence before. His taste, his decisions, his ability to make anything worthwhile out of his life, sure.

But never his expertise.

His expertise let him see the signs.

Tessa's dilated pupils, her still-labored breath and the slight trembling of her limbs made it clear that she was operating under a high level of sexual need.

For him.

His ego took those signs as confirmation that his plan was working.

He had her attention.

With just a taste, he'd started the addiction.

If he fed it too fast, it'd detonate. It'd feel great. But like any one-shot explosion, it'd be done. They'd be done.

Now he just had to tease it out, feed the hunger until she

was starving for more and finesse the spark into a conflagration. And, of course, enjoy the results.

Gabriel's frown slowly shifted into a wicked smile, making Tessa's frown deepen.

Good.

That meant she was confused.

His smile widened as he skimmed his knuckles over the silky warmth of her cheek before sliding his hand into her hair.

Confusion was the point of this particular mission. And as much as he hated leaving a lady disappointed, he was all about the bigger picture here.

He was out to win the war, not just one battle.

No matter how satisfying, how delicious, how carnally incredible that one battle might be.

"You'll love it," he promised in a husky whisper as he skimmed the knuckles of his other hand over her breast, her nipple rock hard and tempting against his skin.

He watched her eyes narrow, the frown edging dangerously close to a scowl. She pulled back, forcing him to release her. She didn't take her eyes off his face as she stepped around him so he had to turn to follow her movements. Tessa leaned sideways to grab one shoe. Without looking, she slipped it onto her foot, then with perfect balance reached down to the other one, too. Gabriel's brows arched, impressed that she'd done all that without even checking left from right. Gotta love a woman who had a knack for doing things by feel alone.

Her delicate feet strapped in those skyscrapers once again, Tessa mounted the first step so they were eye to eye. Hers were about as cold as the ocean behind him, but beneath the irritation there he could still see the heat.

"What d'ya say, angel?" he asked in his most charming tone, fanning those flames. As added incentive, he leaned forward to give her a soft kiss. Given that she was baring her teeth, he considered himself lucky she didn't try to snap his lips off. But hey, he was a SEAL. Never let it be said that he didn't take risks to complete his mission. "Let's go on a date. It'll be fun. We'll move on from a first-name basis and see where it goes."

"Move beyond?" She laughed, shaking her head so that gloriously long mane of hair waved over her breasts, making his mouth water. "Romeo, we're not on a first-name basis now."

"Well, then, we'll change that."

Tessa gave him an assessing look, then stepped to the edge of the stairs. She tucked her finger into his freshly rebuttoned shirt and gave a light tug to pull him closer. Not needing any encouragement, he settled his hands on her hips with a smile.

"There's nothing to change," she told him in a chiding tone, her finger tapping on his chest in time with her words. "Do you know why we refer to each other by nicknames?"

"Everyone refers to me by my nickname," Gabriel said with a laugh.

"You and I, we're a lot alike, Romeo," she pointed out. "We use nicknames to keep people where they belong. At a safe distance so they don't get in our way."

"You're too pretty to be such a cynic," he said with a laugh, pretending her words hadn't hit home.

"I'm a realist, not a cynic," she argued.

"And you're as hot for me as I am for you," he noted, his eyes skimming the rigid peaks of her breasts standing in stark relief against her silk dress. His fingers burned to follow up the look with a caress, but he knew that'd undermine the progress he'd already made. Progress that had come at great physical distress, he admitted, shifting a little to ease the painful pressure of his zipper against his aching erection.

"So?" Tessa challenged with a dismissive shrug. "What's hot got to do with it?"

Appreciating her nod to Tina Turner, he grinned, reaching out to rub her hair between his fingers.

"Now that you've had a taste, you're not going to walk away from this heat between us," he told her confidently. "You might want to. But you won't."

Her eyes flashed, fury so intense he was surprised she wasn't shooting lightning from those blue depths. He could see her jaw clench, but her amused smile didn't shift. God, that control of hers was a turn-on.

"Actually, that's exactly what I am going to do." She tapped her finger against his lips this time before giving him a dismissive smile. "Watch and learn, Romeo. This is what happens when you push a good thing too far."

Those brilliant eyes locked on his for one second longer before Tessa spun on her skyscraper heels and offered him an up-close and not personal enough view of her back, before she sashayed away.

Watching her climb the stairs as if she were out for a casual stroll instead of storming off after a heated rejection, Tessa proved once again that she was in a class by herself.

A very sexy, very tempting class. The silky fabric of her dress swayed in time with those lush hips, cupping her ass with each step. Gabriel had to force himself not to go after her.

He'd see her again, he reminded himself. Their two best friends were not just a couple now, they were a couple hell-bent on nesting. Nesting people did social things that included their friends. And then there was all of the wedding crap Irish had going on.

Yeah. They'd be seeing a lot of each other over the next

little while. He wouldn't have to wait long to see if his gamble had paid off.

Gabriel shoved his hands in his pockets, not an easy feat considering the erection Tessa had left him with. Rocking back on his heels in the sand, he mused that this was the first time in his life that he'd bet against his own talents.

It'd be interesting over the next few weeks to see how many times he'd have to put those talents to the test before being declared the winner.

That he'd win was a sure thing.

Gabriel Thorne never lost.

Especially when it came to the games between the sexes.

5

"IT'S A GAME. It has to be. I mean, what kind of idiot says no to great sex because they're holding out for romance?" Tessa asked, spitting the last word out as if it tasted nasty.

"Me." The response was accompanied by a heavily ringed hand waving absently over a frizz of orange hair, which was all that could be seen of the speaker.

"You actually believe in romance?" Tessa asked, her surprise not slowing her stomp from one end of the office that housed the heart and soul of *Flirtatious* to the other. "Given everything we write about? The relationship statistics? The long-shot odds? Heck, the men you've dated? With all of that data, you're holding out for moonlit lies and sand-castle dreams?"

"It only takes one Mr. Right to beat the odds," Maeve Bannion said absently, her attention still zeroed in on her computer screen. "And I don't put out if he don't put out."

Tessa snorted.

"So you're saying you think guys pay for sex with romance?"

"No more than I think women pay for candlelight dinners, expensive flowers or dancing under the stars with sex."

Tessa frowned, her laughter fading as she thought of the many, many men who figured she'd show her appreciation sexually for being taken to a fancy restaurant or sent lavish gifts. It always seemed so fake to her. She couldn't remember the last romantic date she'd had that wasn't a sad, sad cliché.

She'd written articles on that very theme. Romance by the Numbers: Ten Steps That Work On Every Woman. Or her series called Developing a Signature Style, based on tried and true textbook romantic gestures.

It all came down to bullshit. To spinning the pitch just the right way to achieve the goal. For most men, that was sex. Which brought her back to the question of why waste time with romance?

Tessa's shoulders drooped, her body suddenly feeling as if it weighed a ton.

God, she was jaded. Was that why she shunned romance?

Because she didn't like being disappointed? Because no man had ever moved beyond the textbook steps?

Well, there ya go.

One more thing she didn't want to know about herself.

Tessa sighed, then resumed pacing the room.

She'd spent the entire weekend, ever since Saturday night's engagement party, fuming. She'd tried to work her sexual frustrations off at the gym, and then to bury them in a double-caramel-fudge sundae delight.

Nothing had helped.

She couldn't rant to Livi. Under normal circumstances, her best friend would have been gratifyingly sympathetic, appropriately outraged and completely supportive. But where Romeo was concerned, nothing was normal.

So Tessa had done the next best thing.

She'd hit the office first thing this morning, knowing that her partner would be holed up here obsessing over the specs for the next issue's publication.

"There, in the middle of hot and heavy, the guy turned me down," Tessa grumbled, as irritated at the fact that she, with her excellent verbal skills, had now repeated that same sentence at least nine times as she was with the sentence itself. "Can you believe the arrogant ass?"

"Why?" was all that Maeve muttered, her lanky body hunched over her computer like a gnome over its treasure. A brilliant tech, she'd been wooed by Silicon Valley numerous times. Tessa knew she stayed as much out of loyalty to the company the two women had built with Jared Welch right out of college as it was that Maeve was a woman with strong opinions and strict working-condition requirements.

Which included calling her own hours, insisting on being able to lock her door and ignore everyone until she wanted to talk to them and working barefoot year-round.

Tessa glanced at Maeve's feet, crossed yoga-style on her lap, noting that today's polish was virulent violet with hot pink polka dots.

"*Why?* What do you mean by *why*?" Tessa asked, hoping that somewhere in this conversation, some of Maeve's brilliance would translate into usable advice. Or at least something comprehensible.

"Why is the guy an arrogant ass if he turns down sex? I mean, a woman turns down sex and she's justified. So why is it different for a guy?"

Because no guy had ever turned her down. Tessa kept that fact to herself, settling for sending a scowl at the back of Maeve's head.

"By that logic, he's a tease, then," she said, stabbing her finger in the air as if poking an imaginary Romeo in his very hard, very sculpted chest. "And teases suck."

Maeve sighed. "You ever get going with a guy, thinking it's going to end in hot sex, then for whatever random reason, change your mind?"

Dammit. Tessa growled low in her throat, but couldn't lie. "Of course I have."

Once, she'd walked out on one with his boxers around his ankles. Not because he had a pair of elephant ears tattooed to his upper thighs. But because his *trunk* had been the size of a peanut, he claimed because it was scared of her mouse. Talk about a turnoff.

Wait...

Had she turned off Romeo?

"Do you think there's something wrong with me?" Tessa asked in shock. Feet glued to the floor, she gaped at the back of Maeve's head.

Oh, God. Had Romeo found something wrong with her? The way she kissed? She'd thought he'd been totally into it. His mouth had been wild. Hot and, well, focused. He'd been totally into their kiss, dammit.

So was it her body?

Her knees turned to water at the thought. Her stomach pitched into the toes that were stuck to the floor, before bouncing up into her throat so fast Tessa felt as if she was going to throw up.

It wasn't as if she thought she was God's gift to men, or that she was so conceited to believe herself irresistible. But she'd had enough success with the opposite sex over the years to know that she did hold a certain amount of appeal. Added to that, she made her living writing about the games between the sexes, and statistics supported her belief that men were, generally speaking and given the right circumstances, horndogs who'd do it with anyone who offered.

And their circumstances had been right, dammit.

He'd been into the kiss and hot for her body.

Hadn't he?

Tessa bit her lip, thinking back to Saturday night. Heat swirled through her at the memory, assuring her that any and all of those kisses had been freaking awesome. She had enough experience to know if a guy was faking his reaction, and she knew damned well that her record of no man ever faking with her still stood strong.

"He's playing games," she insisted, as much because she believed it, but also because she really *needed* to believe it. "He has no idea who he's messing with."

Maeve's cackle echoed off her computer monitor. "He's got you good and hooked, so I'd say he knows exactly what he's doing and who he's doing it with."

Her feet finally free again, Tessa resumed pacing.

"That's ridiculous," she railed with a wave of her hand. "I'm not hooked. I'm pissed. There's a difference."

"You walked away from sex," Maeve pointed out, finally turning in her office chair, the cracked black leather creaking in protest as she arched her back and stretched her long arms overhead, bangles clanging together as she did.

Pursing her lips, Tessa debated nitpicking the fact that Romeo was the one who'd turned down sex. But she knew Maeve well enough to know that the minute she did, her friend would point out that he hadn't turned down sex so much as put parameters on what she had to do to get it.

That was the problem bitching to someone as brilliant as Maeve. She was so damned picky about the particulars.

"I walked away from a cliché that was being dangled as a hook to get sex," Tessa explained, ignoring the little voice in the back of her head snickering that it was more as if she'd run away from an emotional temptation with so much weight that if she tried it, it'd sink her.

"Riiight," Maeve drawled. "A cliché. Because that's your deal breaker."

"You've said it yourself a million times," Tessa said, trying to keep the defensive edge out of her tone. "Clichés are lazy."

"In writing. But the cliché of wanting to use romance

as foreplay? That takes an effort. Focus and forethought. Nothin' lazy about that."

What's with all the *F* words? Tessa wanted to add *foreplay* and *fornicate* to the list, but resisted since she knew exactly which word Maeve would shoot back.

"So what's your point?" Tessa asked instead.

"My point is that games can add spice to sex." Maeve arched one slender brow as she uncurled herself from her chair. On her feet she stretched again, her misshapen mustard-colored sweater bagging at the hips of her purple acid-washed jeans. She crossed the office with her mile-eating stride, filled a gallon-size coffee mug with juice from the minifridge. "If you wanted that hot sex, you'd have played it out until you got what you wanted. You always do. Since you ran instead, you might want to ask yourself why."

"I only went for it with the guy to prove something," Tessa muttered. "Why would I prolong that with silly games?"

"That's the end of my advice for the day. Which is why I said ask yourself, not ask me." Maeve curled back into a pretzel in her chair, spinning it to face the computer and resuming her hunched-over position.

And that was that. Maeve was finished humoring her with conversation.

But Tessa wasn't through talking. That was how she figured things out. With words, said out loud, to other people. Except she'd clearly chosen the wrong person to say them to today.

But there was nobody else.

Unable to stand her tangled welter of thoughts but hoping it'd help keep her mouth shut, she started pacing again.

Guys weren't supposed to confuse her.

Since she'd donned her first training bra, she'd had a

firm grip on the male psyche. She'd always seemed to understand what made them tick, why they thought the way they did, what motivated them and where their thoughts were.

Even in those handful of times that their thoughts weren't on sex.

Not that she was a cynic, per se.

Nor was she afraid of the emotional intimacy something like romance could inspire.

Was she?

She'd gone after Romeo because she'd wanted to prove she still had her edge. To show herself that she could handle whatever drama came her way.

And now look at her.

Tessa groaned—actually groaned out loud—as her thoughts tangled together, tripping over themselves in confusion.

Maeve's sigh, dripping with irritation, was a work of art as it echoed through the room.

"Have you told Livi how you feel about this guy?" the other woman asked, her focus on the magazine's layout again instead of Tessa's trek from one end of her office to the other.

"Livi? Are you kidding? She's got stars in her eyes and her ears are filled with cooing doves and giggling cupids," Tessa said with a wave of her hand. "Besides, she likes him. If I tell her what an egotistical creepazoid he is, she might get upset."

"Right." Maeve actually looked up, peering at Tessa over the rim of the funky glasses she'd donned for the close-up work she was doing. Blowing one bright orange corkscrew curl off her nose, she nodded. "Because Livi's not used to you being all forthright and outspoken."

Tessa rolled her eyes at her partner.

"She's pregnant. She never thought she could get pregnant and now she is. Added to that she's all goofy over the baby daddy, she believes that love lasts and she's, you know—" Tessa threw her hands in the air "—Livi."

"Right. Your best friend, the woman you spent last year touring the country with while teaching fitness freaks how to bump and grind their way to weight loss." Maeve made a few more clicks of her mouse without looking at Tessa, then glared at her thirty-inch computer screen before clicking some more. "Weren't you college roommates, too?"

Tessa stopped in front of the floor-length gilt mirror, checking the tuck of her sheer black blouse in the waistband of her pleated leather skirt. She ran her hand over her hair, slicked into its elegant ponytail, before giving Maeve a bland look.

"So?" she asked.

"So I'm pretty sure Livi knows that you're opinionated, hardheaded, sexually aggressive and pleasure oriented."

Well.

Tessa blinked a couple of times, then strolled over to perch her hip on the only clear spot on Maeve's desk. She lifted the stack of cover mock-up boards and tapped them against her knee while giving the other woman a narrow look.

"What?" Maeve asked, when she finally noticed the hard-eyed stare.

"Do I have any other traits you'd like to add to that list?" Tessa asked in her most sardonic tone. "Like maybe that I don't kick puppies or that I'm diligent with my dental care?"

Maeve reached into her high-piled stack of carrot curls and pulled out a pencil, made a note on the ever-present pad of paper at her elbow before sticking the number two back in her hair and giving Tessa a grin. The smile made her look less like grumpy gnome and more like a sexy siren.

"Well, you're also savvy, sophisticated, talented and loyal. But that's not the point. The point is, Livi isn't going to go into shock when she finds out you're hot, horny and hooked on the idea of doing the mattress mambo with her best man."

The only thing that kept Tessa from sliding off the desk in shock was her leather skirt.

"I called the man arrogant and egotistical before listing the many and varied ways he irritates me," she said, trying to ignore the heat in her belly as she imagined doing the mattress mambo—or any other horizontal dance form—with Romeo. "From that you got hot, horny and hooked?"

If forced, she might fess up to the hot and horny. But she'd be damned if she'd admit the hooked part. Even to herself.

"Call it my super skill. I suss these things out." Maeve leaned back in her chair, crossing her arms over her ratty sweater while giving Tessa an impatient look. "You're falling for the guy. So give in to the cliché, do him and get it out of your system. Otherwise get over this crap about protecting Livi by not talking about it."

"I'm sure my system will be fine," Tessa said dismissively. "And why are you pushing me to dump this on Livi?"

"Because you keep trying to talk to me, which is driving me nuts," Maeve said. "In case you haven't noticed in all our years as partners, girly chitchat isn't my thing."

An understatement on par with calling Gabriel Thorne's effect on her body a little interesting.

Tessa had met Maeve in her last year of boarding school, both of them miserably out of place, each for her own reason. They'd bonded over sarcasm and hot chocolate and somehow stayed friends through the years.

So when Maeve had moved back to San Diego after college, one thing had led to another, and pretty soon the two of them and another friend from school—Jared—had launched *Flirtatious*.

"Speaking of, just where is Jared?" Tessa asked, glancing at her watch. They'd had an 8:00 a.m. meeting scheduled and she'd spent most of that hour bitching to Maeve with no sight of Jared.

"Late."

"Late seems to be the new black with him."

"He's up to something," Maeve muttered, her attention sucked back into her computer screen.

"I got that, too," Tessa said with a heavy sigh, not thrilled to have her suspicions confirmed. "How long has this been going on?"

"Since you nabbed the Patrón account. And the Gucci ad. It got worse after the Marriott chain did that string of features."

"He's flaking off because I brought in new accounts?"

Granted, accounts weren't really a part of her job description. She wrote the articles, did interviews, oversaw the freelance columnists. But last year she'd met a lot of influential people during her tour with Livi. Those people turned into contacts, those contacts into contracts.

Which meant more money for the magazine, bigger distribution and better profits. So why would that be a problem?

Maeve's left hand flew over her keyboard while her right danced over the track pad, but Tessa knew her scowl wasn't the result of concentration, or because of the complexity of her work.

"Not flaking, conniving. He's putting in twice as much time, but after hours."

"How do you know that?"

"He's logging on to the server. Pulling financial records for the past two years, running client lists, compiling subscription numbers."

It didn't take Tessa long to add all that to her own suspicions. Her stomach clenched, a million ugly scenarios flashing through her mind.

"He's trying to sell us out?"

"Maybe." Maeve tore her gaze from the computer to give Tessa a long look. "Or throw us under."

Tessa sank into a file-covered chair, ignoring the slide of papers beneath her butt as she tried to think through the problem.

"What do we do? Do we accuse now or watch and wait?" she asked quietly, trying not to put any inflection on either choice. But her mind was screaming watch and wait, watch and wait.

Maeve must have been on the same wavelength, because she just shrugged.

"Nothing to accuse him of yet," she said. "If we jump in now with our women's intuition and a bunch of half-assed suspicions, he'll just bury what he's doing."

"He won't stop, though."

"Nope, just make it harder for us to figure it out."

Tessa nodded. She should be glad, since that put her and Maeve on the same page. But since the page itself sucked, it was hard to work up too much enthusiasm.

"What do we do?" she murmured, feeling lost.

"Like you said, watch and wait. Forearmed and all that," Maeve said with a shrug. "Guess we each need to figure out what we're going to do when things change."

That they would change went without saying.

MAEVE'S WORDS WERE still playing through Tessa's mind when she rode the elevator up to Livi's apartment that evening. It wasn't that she didn't enjoy change. She just preferred to be the one initiating it. Which meant she always made sure to initiate it in small, easily assimilated bits.

Not in a giant swoop of change pouring through her life like a huge wave, wiping out every damned thing all at once. Between the problems at *Flirtatious*, the changes with Livi and feeling as if she were losing her sexual mojo thanks to Romeo, Tessa was on complete overload. One more change, even something as simple as hearing that they were repaving the parking lot at her apartment, and she was pretty sure she'd run screaming into the night with her head on fire.

And, oh, God, when had she become such a drama queen?

Tessa let her thankfully fire-free head rest on the elevator wall as she took a few deep breaths and tried to settle her crazy thoughts into some semblance of order. The last thing Livi needed was one of her dinner guests showing up stressed out.

Especially not if the other dinner guest was part of the cause of that stress. Tessa might be frazzled and prone to drama, but she reminded herself that she was also an expert on men. And because she was, she would make sure that Romeo didn't get the better of her two visits in a row.

With that in mind she straightened, and this time her deep breaths were cleansing ones.

In with the confidence, out with the worries.

In with the sexy energy, out with the stress.

In with the attractive mojo, out with the self-doubts.

And one last breath to perk up her breasts and bring a little color to her cheeks and that was it. Tessa was ready when the elevator dinged.

Stepping into the hallway, her hips were back to swinging and her easy smile was in place. She strode toward Livi's door, certain that she wasn't carrying any of her crap with her.

At least, not on the surface, where anyone—not even her best friend—would notice it.

"Mitch, hello," she greeted with a friendly smile when he opened the door. "I brought wine and a present."

"I'd say you shouldn't have, but Livi would hurt me. You know how she loves presents," he said, his blue eyes laughing before he ushered her into the apartment.

Tessa hadn't been there in a couple of weeks, not since the couple had announced their engagement, but she knew that Mitch was pretty much living here when he wasn't on base. She followed him inside, stopping where the entry opened into the living area.

She didn't realize how much she'd been dreading seeing it until the knot in her stomach unraveled. Nothing had changed. Not really. The large, airy apartment was still filled with soothing shades of blue and purple. The sunken living area was a sea of white furniture and carpeting, accented with blown glass, rich throws and clever knickknacks.

A vivid contrast to Tessa's own apartment. Her place screamed of sensual luxury, with its jewel tones and cool surfaces, where Livi's space was soothing and peaceful. Things Tessa rarely felt, almost never sought. Probably because she knew that kind of serenity was always here for her if she needed it.

Would that change now?

Would she still be welcome to come and go as she pleased, to make this haven her own second home? Where would she fit once Livi and Mitch settled into their new life, wrapped around their new priorities? They'd be happy, she hoped. But how long would she be invited to see that happiness?

"I heard the word *present*," Livi said, coming out of the kitchen and wiping her hands on a towel before wrapping her arms around Tessa in a welcoming hug.

Grateful for the distraction from what was becoming an all-too-familiar sense of self-pity, Tessa returned the hug with a tight squeeze.

"Gimme," Livi teased with a bright smile when she'd stepped back.

"Who said it was for you?" Tessa asked, wide-eyed. She handed a grinning Mitch the bottle of wine, then dangled the gift bag by its satin handles so that the purple foil caught the light. Then, laughing, she handed it to Livi.

Without ceremony, teal tissue flew one way, then the bag the other before her friend gave a broken exclamation.

"Are you okay?" Mitch asked, hurrying from the kitchen when his fiancée burst into tears. He pulled Livi into his arms, shooting Tessa a dark look. "What'd you give her?"

"Happy tears," Livi explained, patting his shoulder.

"You need a warning sign," he muttered, shaking his head. But Tessa saw the look on his face and knew that he'd have come running just as quickly for happy tears as he would for sad. Clearly, the man would break the four-minute mile for love.

"Look," Livi said, holding up the plush octopus. The watercoloresque fabric poured purples into blues into sea foam and back, with the happy-faced sea denizen wearing its own little sailor hat. "Isn't it darling?"

Mitch's smile turned goofy as he took the toy and examined it. Then, without warning, he pulled Tessa into a hug of his own, giving her a quick, friendly squeeze.

"Thank you," he said before handing Livi back the toy with a kiss.

"I know you said you hadn't decided on a theme or colors for the nursery, but I couldn't resist," she said, running her fingertip over one soft leg.

"He's perfect. It's perfect," Livi murmured, leaning her head on Mitch's shoulder as they both gazed at the octopus as if it offered insights into the joys of their future.

Ignoring the empty feeling in her stomach, Tessa gave another quick look around the apartment, even though she knew Romeo wasn't lurking there somewhere.

"So," Tessa said brightly, her smile only a little stiff. "How about some wine? Then you can tell me all about the latest workout filming while I help you with dinner."

She'd almost said, "When your other dinner guest would arrive," but managed to change her words at the last moment. She didn't want anyone thinking she wanted to see him. She'd just keep it to herself that her stomach was doing little loop-de-loops.

"Wine coming up," Mitch promised with one last kiss to the top of Livi's head before he headed for the kitchen.

Tessa followed Livi around the small wall that separated the entry and kitchen from the dining area and living room, listening to her friend rhapsodize about her latest workout program as they went. Her eyes landed on the teak table and she frowned. Around the artistic arrangement of yellow and indigo flowers were only three settings.

Romeo wouldn't be joining them.

She almost tripped over her own toes at the realization.

Relief, she promised herself. That flood of emotion pouring through her was pure relief. Now she could relax as she tried to find her place in this new mix that was her best friend's life.

She smiled as she settled onto her usual place on the

couch and accepted Mitch's proffered glass of wine with a murmur of thanks.

She was glad Romeo wasn't here. It was better this way. Who needed a whole bunch of sexual tension, hot looks and sizzling desires messing up dinner?

Certainly not her, she assured herself.

Then, sipping her wine, she wondered when she'd sunk so low that she'd started lying to herself. Probably when she'd peeled her body away from the delicious temptation of Romeo's.

6

GABRIEL WAS A man who'd been raised to understand that life moved in stages. The seasons, the years. Trainings, missions, procedures—they all followed a cycle. He understood the value of those cycles, the need to layer the necessary steps in the right order to achieve a desired outcome.

Over the years, people had expressed surprise that a man who blew things up for a living could be so chill in his belief that things happened when they were meant to and not a moment before. But he'd learned that trying to circumvent the right timing was usually a recipe for disaster. But Gabriel's patience was an innate part of his thought process, as natural as breathing and as deep as his faith that everything happened for a reason.

So it was a rare and unwelcome thing to find that patience dangling by one loose thread, ready to snap at any second.

It was even rarer that he was willing to risk that thread by using it to strangle someone. But today, he was more than ready to lose the rare power of his temper, and let it explode all to hell on one particular person.

Jeglinski.

But...

Gabriel shifted the pretty pink box from one hand to the other, leaning his shoulder against the wall of the elevator as he took a deep, calming breath.

He wouldn't.

It took the rest of the elevator ride for him to believe

that. But when the metal box dinged, he set his irritation aside and buried his anger, and his usual mellow facade was solidly in place.

By the time he reached Livi's door, his smile was comfortable, his charm in place and his mood upbeat. So when the pretty blonde welcomed him in, he was able to hold up the dessert box and wiggle his brows suggestively.

"What, I wonder, would a pregnant lady do for a delicious dessert?" he mused.

"Gabriel," Livi exclaimed, throwing her arms around him.

With his usual lightning reflexes, Gabriel lifted the box overhead, where it wasn't in danger of being jostled or squashed, even as his other arm came around to return her hug.

"Wow, you must have one major sweet tooth," he teased.

"More like I was worried when you canceled dinner," Livi told him, her voice lowering as she shifted back to inspect his face. "Mitch said it was no big deal, but he had that voice when he said it. You know, the totally casual, completely innocuous voice? So I knew it was."

Gabriel wondered what it was like to have someone read you so easily. Irish was one of the best, had been courted by the powers that be to serve on DEVGRU. He wasn't easy to read. Love must be pretty special if it gave those kind of insights.

"And you didn't nag him into telling?" Gabriel teased. "You are a queen among women, Ms. Kane."

"Oh, no," Livi said, her voice still low as she sent a quick look over her shoulder. "I didn't let on that I knew. It'd just upset him, then he'd worry about me. Then I'd worry about him worrying about me, in addition to me already worrying about you."

His mind spinning as he tried to follow that, Gabriel decided he was much better off without having anyone read him. That sounded like way too much worry for his taste.

"Come in," she invited, taking the box and curling her arms around it protectively "You're just in time for coffee."

"Coffee sounds great."

He entered the apartment to another great sound.

Tessa's laughter.

Gabriel's grin turned wicked.

Time for another round of Operation Romance.

"Dessert delivery?" he heard Tessa say in a delighted tone. "You had dessert specially delivered?"

"There's this great place in Virginia that makes these custom éclairs. Livi had one when we were back visiting my mom a few weeks ago and she's been craving them ever since. So I had some flown in."

"What are you going to do in a few months if she's craving some exotic condiment from Turkey?" Tessa asked with a laugh.

"I know people. I'm sure I can fly those in, too."

Gabriel stepped into the room just in time to see the goofy look on Irish's face over the idea that his gal was getting cravings.

Before he could laugh, his gaze was caught by the gorgeous angel seated on the couch. Lust hit like a fist to the gut at the vision she made, her hair pulled back to leave her lovely face unframed. Her sheer black blouse emphasized rather than hid her black bra and flat abs, while her black skirt looked like something a cheerleader would wear. He rocked back on the heels of his motorcycle boots, grinning. A *naughty* cheerleader.

"Hello, angel," he greeted.

Her eyes flashed. But for the first time it wasn't irritation he saw in those big blue depths. If he wasn't mistaken—and he never was about these things—it was interest.

The triumph was brief. He knew he hadn't won the war. But he was still taking this as a tactical victory. And like any good victory, he planned to parlay it into a bigger win with carefully orchestrated, strategic steps.

Ready to get started, he stepped farther into the room and turned his attention to Irish.

"Commander," he greeted with a modified salute.

"Romeo," Mitch responded, rising to shake his hand. "Thanks for making the trip. How was the flight?"

Knowing his commander was asking about more than the condition of the travel from the East Coast to West, he glanced at Mitch, shrugging to indicate that the mission was proceeding according to plan. He'd spent the past thirty hours in Little Creek being briefed in the use of the new bomb gear.

Satisfied with his report, such as it was, Mitch nodded, then tilted his head to indicate Gabriel be at ease.

"Can I get you a beer?" Irish offered.

"Sure." Free now to indulge in the next stage of his plan, Gabriel stepped into the sunken living area and gave Tessa a smile. The kind he'd offer a friend's mother or an elderly shop clerk. Nonthreatening, nonsexual and friendly.

Instead of taking a seat next to Tessa on the couch, or even in the chair opposite, where he could stare directly at her, he took the chair to her right.

Damn, she had a great profile.

He watched with appreciation as she gave a deep sigh, the move pressing her breasts tighter against the sheer fabric of her blouse. Then, as if she couldn't stand it any longer, she turned her head and gave him a cool look under arched brows.

"Here ya go, Romeo," Irish said.

Gabriel reached out to take the bottle, but he didn't take his eyes off the black-haired beauty staring at him.

He couldn't read her gaze. He knew he hadn't imagined the interest he'd seen there earlier, and he didn't doubt for a second that she could wield indifference with deadly accuracy.

Which meant she was hiding the interest.

His smile widened.

Operation Romance was working just fine. He'd gotten her attention the other night with his opening salvo of a kiss. He'd issued his terms. Now the fun could start. Keeping her off balance enough that she didn't lose interest, but not letting things get so out of hand that he couldn't resist giving in. He'd wait her out, see how long it took before she couldn't resist talking to him.

"Oh, Gabriel, these look amazing."

It wasn't Livi's gushing exclamation that freed his attention. It was that her words seemed to flip a switch for Tessa. With just a flick of her lashes, the brunette angel dismissed him to turn her gaze toward her friend. His lips twitched as the message came through loud and clear.

Shoo, those lashes said. *Just shoo.*

Damn, she was cute the way she thought she had the upper hand.

"Tessa, aren't they decadent looking?" Livi said as she set a tray on the glass coffee table. "My mouth is already watering."

"They look great," Tessa acknowledged, accepting the plate Livi offered and sending Mitch a teasing smile. "I didn't know you were craving éclairs, though. I thought you were on a kale kick."

"Balance. It's all about balance," Livi said with a wave of her hand. "I had this sudden craving for cream-filled pastries last night, but there were no good bakeries open at midnight. I finally settled for hot cocoa and whipped cream, but it wasn't the same."

"You should have told me you were in the mood for something besides seaweed," Tessa said. "I'd have stopped at the little bakery by my place that you love."

"That's okay," Livi said as she handed Mitch his plate, along with a kiss. "Mitch said he'd get them for me."

Hurt flashed in Tessa's eyes but was hidden away with another whisk of those lashes. He frowned. More interested in knowing the cause than in his plan to wait for her to speak first, Gabriel planted his elbows on his knees, his fingers loosely linked between them as he leaned forward.

"So did you offer to bring Livi kale, too?" he asked.

Tessa lifted her gaze from her plate to give him a sardonic look.

"Friendship has its limits," she declared. "Seaweed is one of them."

"Now, that's not true," Livi said, finally tearing her attention off her fiancé to give her friend a wide-eyed look. "You found me kale in Albuquerque."

"You were chewing on your fingernails," Tessa pointed out, circling her fork in the air. "I had to get you something to calm your nerves."

Livi wrinkled her nose before giving Gabriel a rueful smile.

"We were doing a tour to promote my Strip Fit workout program and I used to have a little trouble facing crowds. Tessa was always great at keeping me focused before events, but she had a major deadline when we hit Albuquerque so I had to go it alone."

Tessa's lips twitched.

"I got there a half hour before the second workout," Tessa explained, curling her feet under her as she got more comfy. This was about as relaxed as Gabriel had ever seen the petite powerhouse. "Apparently she'd white-knuckled it through the first session. Now she's got two hundred people waiting in a stadium while she's pacing this makeshift stage, muttering the lyrics to 'Pour Some Sugar On Me' and chewing her nails off. I had to do something before she ran out of fingers and went for the toes."

Gabriel could see the history of affection in the look the women shared before Livi shook her head at the memory.

"Tessa knew the best thing to calm me down was food, but I was about to go on stage wearing the equivalent of a sequined bikini. Comfort food was out of the question—"

"Normal-people comfort food was out," Tessa interrupted, rolling her eyes toward the men and pulling a face. "But I knew Ms. Fit here could be soothed with some twigs or leaves or, you know, seaweed."

"So she grabbed a cab, found the nearest health food store and filled a grocery bag with everything health food," Livi laughed. "I still don't know how you managed to do all of that and get back before the session began."

"Pl-ee-ase." Tessa drew the word out, her expression sliding from light and amused to seductively sultry with just a flick of her lashes. "The cabbie was a man."

Even as he joined the others' laughter, Gabriel mentally filed the insight that comment offered, patting himself on the back for his plan to play it cool. She was so used to guys falling all over her, but he wondered if any of them actually saw her for more than a sexy body and gorgeous face.

His laugh fading into a frown, Gabriel realized that he wasn't any better.

He was busy pondering that when Livi offered him the cream-filled, chocolate-covered delicacy.

"No, thanks." He shook his head. "You can have my share."

"You don't eat sweets?"

"I never deprive a beautiful woman of an extra helping of anything that makes her smile," he said.

As Livi's expression melted in delight, he saw Tessa roll her eyes. But she looked more amused than disdainful, so he figured he was making progress. He just wasn't as sure now what he wanted to progress toward. He didn't want to be just another horndog with a hard-on scheming his way into her bed.

"Ooh," Livi said with a soft moan as she ate her first bite. She arched her brows at Tessa and gestured with another forkful. "Mitch was right. This is delicious. Like, totally worth an extra twenty minutes of cardio."

"You eat that second one and you might need to up that to sixty," Tessa said with a laugh.

"Do you ladies really do that?" Mitch asked. "Seriously measure each bite in terms of how much exercise you'll have to do after eating it?"

"While I'm filming I do." Livi gave Gabriel's rejected plate a woeful look, then licked her fork. "I'm not as obsessive about it now as I was before, but I'm still careful. But that's me. Tessa here burns through calories as if they're air. I think she just works out to keep me company."

"Metabolism," Tessa intoned in a low, sexy voice, toasting with her fork.

"You and your metabolism. I'd hate you for it if you didn't have to work so hard for muscle tone," Livi said teasingly.

"We all have our challenges," Tessa acknowledged seriously before grinning. The smile lit up her face with a sense of fun that Gabriel hadn't realized she had. He leaned back in his chair, deliberately making himself unobtrusive—another carefully honed talent that came both through blood and years of training.

He was fascinated by Tessa in this mood and didn't

want to do anything to bring her out of it. He wondered if light and easy was something she reserved for Livi, or if it was the dessert bringing it out in her.

"I've seen women cry when they see how this one eats," Livi told them, gesturing with her fork to Tessa, whose dessert plate was already sparkling clean. "The only thing they hate worse is that she never gets drunk."

"Never?" Mitch asked, his tone showing the same surprise Gabriel felt.

He'd seen her drink, so knew she wasn't a teetotaler.

"Is that another credit to your metabolism?" Mitch asked.

"Not really." Tessa leaned forward to set her plate on the table, her eyes sliding to Gabriel for the first time since he'd walked into the room. "It's more a testament to my determination to stay in control. Alcohol has a way of making people do stupid things they end up regretting later."

"Or it gets rid of those inhibitions that keep them from doing the things they really want," Gabriel suggested.

"If someone wants to do something, they do it," she argued, her tone still friendly. "It'd be a sad way to go through life if one needed excuses in order to let themselves have a good time, don't you think?"

"Well, what I really want is coffee," Livi declared in a cheery tone. Whether she was seriously needing a caffeine fix or if she just wanted to get out of the line of fire, Gabriel didn't know. But she gathered the plates and headed for the kitchen with Irish in tow pretty damned fast.

Never able to ignore a challenge, Gabriel set his plan aside and offered Tessa a slow smile that said he knew exactly what she was doing, but was more than willing to play.

"What's worse?" he asked in a musing tone as he gave in to the need and looked her over from head to foot. He'd never known a more beautiful woman. Or one he craved so desperately. Figuring a little honesty would impress her more than games, he tilted his head. "Excuses in order to have a good time? Or excuses to run from one?"

"I SUPPOSED IT'S all perspective," Tessa said with a slow, meandering inspection of her own. Damn, the man was gorgeous. From the tip of his closely shorn black hair to the toes of his impressively large boots, he was a study in, well, studliness. The little black cloud that'd been hovering over Tessa's mood didn't stand a chance against Romeo's appeal. "One person's excuse is another person's reality after all."

"Nicely put," he said with an impressed nod. "Philosophical, fair and completely reasonable."

Tessa gave a regal inclination of her head.

"And totally bullshit," he added, making her burst into laughter.

"You're calling bullshit on my reasonable philosophy?"

"I think I am. You see, we're a lot alike, you and me." He waited a beat, as if giving her an opening to object. But Tessa didn't see any point arguing with the truth. His dark eyes glinted at her silence, then he continued. "You and I, angel, we're damned good at doing what we're good at."

"Oh, now, there's a philosophical statement," she teased.

"We're good at taking a challenge and making it our own," he said quietly, his tone reflective. And so nonthreatening that she found herself nodding.

"We live on our own terms. We embrace what feels right. And we ignore what doesn't."

Not sure why she felt so at ease with him sitting there reading her as if she was a book, Tessa found herself nodding again. Maybe she was comfortable with it because they were both on the same page. All he was doing was stating simple facts, and those facts would work just fine when she turned them around on him to support her refusing to play his little pay-for-sex-with-romance game.

"I'm still not hearing anything that makes my philosophy bullshit," she pointed out with a sweet smile. Then, as much to get more comfortable as to tease him a little, she shifted her legs up onto the couch and slid her bare feet under her butt, the pleats of her leather skirt fanning out over her thighs.

Romeo's eyes darkened, his gaze a hot caress as it trailed over her legs before giving her an appreciative smile.

"We're experts at what we do," he continued, his voice a half decibel lower. "So good, in fact, that we tend to be so used to our skills that we take them for granted."

Tessa's brow creased a little. Did she take things for granted? Maybe she'd gotten so used to having life just the way she wanted it that she had.

"The problem with taking things for granted is we don't appreciate them the way they should be," he said, as if reading her mind. He leaned forward. Tessa barely stopped herself from leaning in to meet him.

"Since I'm an expert, I know better than to tell you that you're the sexiest woman I've ever known. I know you're so used to men falling all over you that you wouldn't appreciate my telling you that I'm so fascinated by your lips that I can't forget their taste. The feel of them beneath mine is stuck in my memory, and even if I could dislodge it, I wouldn't."

Remembering their kisses, Tessa had to swallow twice before she could wet those lips.

"But if I told you that, you'd pull out one of those excuses of yours. Probably something about the predictability of men, how I had my chance and blew it. Then you'd saunter away, wondering why men were so stuck on your looks that they never saw you as a person," he said with a shrug.

Tessa shifted, all of that discomfort she'd wondered about hitting her like a brick wall. Just a lucky guess, she told herself. It wasn't as if he knew her that well.

"So I definitely wouldn't tell you what I'd like to do the next time I get my lips on you. How I'd like to spend at least an hour with those lips before I slide my mouth over the delicate length of your throat. How I'd breathe in your scent, letting it wrap around me like an aphrodisiac."

Tessa took a deep breath through her nose. She was too used to her own perfume to smell it, but she could breathe in the scent of Romeo. Like the ocean, it was light and clean with undertones of something dangerous. Yeah. She could imagine some women—more gullible than she— thinking it was an aphrodisiac. There was something sexy about his scent that reached deep into her belly and stirred her desires.

"But when I breathe you in, I forget things like excuses and expertise. All I can think of is finding your pleasure zones."

How'd he do that? One second he'd been talking philosophy, the next he was verbally seducing her. Tessa's pulse raced, her body humming with awareness. A few words and one look and he had her so close to the edge.

Worried she was losing control—of the conversation, of the relationship and of her own body's reaction—Tessa grasped for some of that expertise he'd mentioned and shot him a look. She was going for arch disdain, but was afraid it was closer to eager curiosity.

"Pleasure zones?" she said, tapping her fingers on her knee as if she were bored. Or, in this case, trying to subtly shake off some of the sexual overload. "So, what? Your expertise extends to discovering new erogenous zones? Aren't you clever."

He flashed a grin, fast and appreciative, before he shook his head.

"I have to admit, I'm not one of those guys who thinks that women are interchangeable," he said in the tone of a man confessing a horrible fault. "I figure every woman's pleasure zone is as unique as she is."

"Mmm, I'll bet you score big-time with that pickup line." Tessa arched one brow, pretending she hadn't had to swallow a couple of times to push her words past her tight throat.

"Please. Do you think I need pickup lines?" He gave her a look that would have been arrogance on any other man's face. But on Romeo it simply bespoke a confidence based on experience.

She shifted uncomfortably, disturbed at how alike they really were.

"I don't need gimmicks any more than I need a generic map of a woman's erogenous zones," he continued, his voice a little lower, whether because he didn't want to be overheard, or because he wanted her to lean in closer to hear him, she wasn't sure.

Tessa stubbornly leaned back.

"Pleasure zones rely on combinations. For instance, I already know you like your kisses hard and long. You are all about the thrust of my tongue over yours, our lips sliding together."

She pressed her lips together tightly.

"But what I don't know is where you'd like to be touched while I kiss you," he mused. "Do you want me to grab your butt, squeezing as I pull you tight against my body? Or do you prefer something softer, a gentle graze of my fingers over your breasts while we kiss?"

Her nipples peaked, hard and stiff. Tessa took a deep breath, the thick satin of her bra rubbing erotically against the tender flesh.

"Or maybe you'd rather I grab your wrists, holding them overhead with one hand while I kiss your neck, just there, where it meets the curve of your shoulder. With my free hand I'd squeeze your breast, my thumb working your nipple into a stiff peak."

Holy mother of pleasure. Tessa swallowed hard to keep from moaning. His words were hypnotic, as powerful as if he were really touching her. Need coiled, low and tight in her belly. Her pulse jumped and her mouth went dry at the look on his face. That was how he'd look if he were poised over her, his powerful body thrusting into her welcoming heat.

"Or maybe we'd go a little slower," he said, his voice more intense, more demanding. "I might try grazing your nipples with my lips while my palms skim over your skin, teasing and tempting along your waist, down to your thighs. I'd slip my fingers into your heat."

As if he'd done just that, her heat trembled. She clenched her thighs tight, struggling not to wiggle or squirm. She'd always heard counting backward or reciting the Gettysburg Address worked to delay an orgasm. She didn't know that it'd delay it long enough for her to get home to the privacy of her bedroom. But she'd take a minute or two, enough time for her to either derail this little verbal seduction, for the coffee fairies to interrupt it or for a miracle to happen and Romeo say the wrong thing.

"I'd want to start slow, just rubbing your bud between my fingers while I suck your nipple into my mouth," he said, his words so quiet now they were almost a growl. "But as soon as I knew how you liked it, I'd intensify my focus. I'd plunge my finger inside you, work you with my thumb, tease you with my tongue."

Tessa didn't get past the forefathers bringing forth the nation before she felt it. That tiny ping of passion's coil springing free. Her orgasm was fast and sweet, a quick pop of pleasure that burst through her system. Her gasp was barely an inhalation, but she knew Romeo was as aware of her climax as she was.

For the first time in her life, she felt a little embarrassed by her sexual response. All he'd done was talk. And not even dirty talk. And poof, she'd come in a burst of pleasure. She'd never gone up so easily.

It took a couple of seconds for her to level out her system. Her thighs stopped trembling, but her nipples still ached, and her pulse was bouncing around like a rubber ball.

"That's why all of your philosophy, any of your excuses won't matter." Romeo's eyes were molten with satisfaction, as if he'd taken as much pleasure from her orgasm as she had. "They won't stop the inevitable."

"And what's the inevitable?" she breathed, even though she was pretty sure of the answer.

"Us, together. Sex, wild and uncontrolled. Passion, hot and intense. Sooner or later, it'll happen," he promised. "It's inevitable."

"There's more to the decision to have sex than the simple pursuit of pleasure," she insisted. A little voice in the back of her head taunted her for being a hypocrite, but she ignored it. "But seeing as you're such an expert, I'm sure you already know that."

It was a lousy comeback, but with her body still trembling and her brain on meltdown, it was the best she could do.

Desperate for control, wishing she could grab a little of

her pride back, Tessa gave him a dismissive look. Then, taking her time, she gracefully slid to her feet and headed for the kitchen to hurry up the coffee.

It was that or prove herself a liar and jump him.

7

TESSA PACED THE length of her bedroom, the lush carpet sinking beneath her bare toes with every step. The room was an ode to sensuality, from the satin headboard to the velvet pillows, from the bleeding hues of reds and purples to the art deco nudes gracing the walls. Roses poured out of an ice pick of a vase, the scent rich and seductive.

Usually, the bedroom was Tessa's haven. Just stepping through the door brought her relaxation.

Except tonight.

She blamed Romeo.

It'd been two days. Two whole, entire days, and she still couldn't believe he'd gotten her off so quickly, so easily. Under five minutes, with words alone. While their friends were in the other room making coffee, no less.

Tessa shoved her hands into her hair, grabbed a couple of fistfuls and tugged. But that didn't change the facts.

It'd been good.

Damned good.

The heady warmth of remembered pleasure trickled through her body, assuring her that yes, indeed, that'd been one hell of an orgasm.

And then what had he done? Had he tried to convince her to take him home afterward? Had he flirted through coffee or make any sexual innuendos?

No.

He'd made a few minutes of friendly conversation, offered some lame excuse and left.

All he'd said to her was that he'd be in touch.

What the hell was wrong with him?

And what had he meant when he'd said he'd be in touch? Did he plan to stop by her place?

She stopped in the doorway, resisting the urge to hurry out and make sure the apartment was tidy. And, more important, that there was nothing emotionally incriminating for him to see.

Like the stuffed bunny she'd kept since childhood, or any of the notes to herself she usually stuck on the refrigerator door with reminders like "cheer up" or "buy yourself flowers, you deserve it." Or worse, the graduation photo of her and her mom—one of the few shots Tessa had with her mother that didn't feature any of her men of the month.

Biting her lip, she almost hurried out to hide them away. Then she stopped herself.

He wasn't coming here.

She was sure he was off somewhere, doing military things like marching or maybe swimming, since he was a SEAL. He'd only said he'd be in touch because he wanted to make her nervous. It was a game. A lame attempt to make sure she kept thinking about him.

As if she needed any reminders of what he'd done. Or of the way his lips curved into a wicked smile to match the angle of those razor-sharp cheekbones. Lips like that were unforgettable. Sexy and tempting all by themselves, but even more memorable when they were attached to that body.

Tessa puffed out a breath, her heart dancing a little faster as images of that body flashed through her mind.

And, oh, what a body it was.

Between her job, her work with Livi in the fitness field and her extensive personal experience with men, Tessa had seen plenty of sexy men. But none seemed to have the perfect combination that Romeo had.

From the muscled breadth of his shoulders down to those rock-hard biceps. Oh, the biceps. Tessa paused the mental journey for a second to give a deep sigh of appreciation for the glory that was Romeo's biceps.

The man was seriously built. The only thing better than his biceps was his ass. Such a sweet ass. The kind that'd fit just right in her hands, waiting to be squeezed, or gripped by her fingers while he thrust into the waiting heat of her body.

Or maybe his smile. She'd bet he flashed women that same wicked smile when he was stripping his clothes off that sexy body. Did he smile when he slid his body over a woman's? Or did he get that intense, serious look she'd seen in his eyes every once in a while? That was the look that made him so dangerous.

When he turned it her way, she knew he could see all the way into her most secret desires, that he knew her deepest, darkest needs. Needs that she'd never had fulfilled, never trusted a man enough to share. Would Romeo know how to do her right?

She'd bet he would.

She skimmed her palm over her breast, the tip pebbled with need and tingling at her touch. Heat coiled, wet and needy in her belly. Lips pursed, she glanced at her bedside table with its drawer full of satisfaction.

All it'd take was a quick spin with one of her battery-operated toy friends and she'd be loose with pleasure.

But as much as she wanted the satisfaction, she resisted. Her body was so tight it probably wouldn't even take batteries to send her over the edge. But if she came because she was all hot for Romeo, it'd be as though she was dedicating her orgasm to him.

Tessa shook her head at the ridiculousness of that idea. But after another yearning glance at the drawer, she decided to take her pacing to the living room.

Not bothering with a robe, she side tripped into the kitchen wearing just a ruffled nighty, the soft white linen floating around her as she poured herself a glass of wine.

She just needed sex.

A fast, hot roll between the sheets, a few orgasms for two, maybe a bone-melting body slam against a wall.

Easy enough. All it'd take was a guy.

Tessa sighed, then took a medicinal gulp of wine.

The problem was, she only wanted one guy.

She couldn't have sex with some other guy while she was fantasizing about Romeo. That'd just be wrong.

Not just because she had a policy against having sex with a man if he wasn't good enough to put all fantasies out of her mind for the duration.

Nor because she didn't think it was fair to use a guy as a sex substitute. Not that most guys would care, but that wasn't the point.

She couldn't do it because she was pretty sure that all it would do was make her want Romeo more. It would be like craving an ice cream sundae and settling for a sugar-free Popsicle.

She knew most people thought that because she was so sexually confident, she slept with anyone, anytime. That she was having sex five nights a week, juggling partners as if they were circus tricks or that she had to change partners like other people changed sheets because she was so jaded.

Wouldn't they be shocked to find out she hadn't had sex in six months.

Tapping her fingers on the black granite countertop, Tessa frowned at her wine. Had it really been six months without sex?

Who was she?

She felt as though she didn't even know anymore.

Feeling a little sick to her stomach, Tessa drained the rest of her wine. She deliberately set the glass on the kitchen counter and walked out of the kitchen before she was tempted to go for a refill.

Because if a sexless six months weren't enough to make a girl want to drink, all of these stupid self-doubts definitely were.

She started pacing again, feeling lost in her own living room as she tried to sort through the weltering mess of emotions knotted in her stomach.

She'd never been so grateful to hear a telephone ring.

It was either Livi or Maeve. Nobody else ever called her this late. She grabbed the phone midpace and answered without checking the display.

"Distract me," she said instead of offering a greeting. She'd take any distraction—even if it was techno-babble. Or worse, another endless debate over the merits of roses versus lilies in a bridal bouquet.

"Hello, angel. That's a difficult offer to resist."

"Romeo?"

Talk about a distraction. Her lips curved before she could stop them, heat curling low in her belly at the sound of his voice. How long was she supposed to resist a man who could get her wet and ready with just a few well-chosen words?

Tessa's smile gave way to a sigh.

Was that why he was calling? To pick up where he'd left off two days ago? A little phone sex?

"It's a little late to be calling," she said, suspicion adding a chill to her tone.

"It's barely ten in your time zone," he said, his shrug coming through clearly, even over the phone line.

"My time zone? Does that mean they've booted you out of Coronado already?" She should be glad. If he didn't live nearby, those little dessert treats at Livi and Mitch's would be few and far between. But the feeling in her stomach felt more like disappointment than happiness.

"Nah, they love me in California." His words were light, the tone easy and fun, but there was an edge there. "I'm doing some training somewhere else, though."

Training for a mission?

Tessa sank onto her couch, pulling a pillow close to hug to her chest. She wanted to ask if it was dangerous, but she was pretty sure most everything the SEALs did was probably dangerous.

"Why are you calling?" she asked, both to distract her sudden worries and because she was genuinely curious.

"I told you I'd be in touch. Consider this me, touching..." His pause was so loaded with sexual power that Tessa wouldn't be surprised if the phone melted. Then he continued in his usual tone, "Base."

"Touching base?"

"You know, talk. Have a conversation. See what's going on and what you've been up to."

She'd just bet that was what this was about.

"You're calling to chat," she repeated, disguising her surprise with a heavy coating of sarcasm. "As if we're, what? Girlfriends?"

He laughed.

"Did you want to be my girlfriend?"

"You might not have noticed, but I'm a woman," she proclaimed in an arch tone, ignoring the fact that she'd used the word *girl* first.

"Believe me, I noticed. A man would have to be dead a year to not notice." Before she could make a clever comeback, he asked, "Have you seen Livi since the éclairs the other night?"

"Livi?" Surprised, Tessa sat on the leather arm of the couch, frowning in the dark. "I had lunch with her yesterday. Why? Is something wrong?"

"Nope, just wondering if you'd seen that picture the doctor sent home with her and Irish."

"The sonogram?" Tessa slid from the arm of the couch onto the cushion. Livi had said everything was fine.

"Yeah, that's what Irish called it. Something to do with an ultrasound."

"What about it?" Hurt and worry tangled together as Tessa wondered what Livi hadn't told her. She understood that Mitch would know; he was the baby daddy. But why would Livi keep news from her? Especially bad news. Weren't they best friends?

"Did you understand it?"

Tessa blinked a couple of times as she tried to process that question.

"Did I understand what? The picture?" Not quite past the anxiety attack he'd inspired, Tessa frowned. "I think it's made with sound waves or something."

"Angel, I spend a lot of my time on a submarine. I'm trained in sonar. And I still couldn't find the baby in that picture." He sounded so frustrated.

She bit her lip to keep from laughing.

"I think it's sort of like those *Magic Eye* picture books. Did you ever look at those when you were a kid? You have to relax your eyes and let the page blur to see the actual image."

"I wasn't much into reading as a kid," he admitted. "But if training in sonar didn't help, I doubt a picture book would."

He sounded so frustrated. Since nobody was there to

see her, Tessa grinned. Snuggling deeper into the couch, she pulled the cashmere throw from the back and tucked it around herself.

"So what did you say if you couldn't see the baby?" she asked.

"I asked if it had a penis, of course."

With a burst of laughter, she accused, "You did not."

"Hey, that's what guys want to know. We're all about the equipment."

Pretty sure that talking about his equipment while sitting in the dark was not a good idea, Tessa just hummed.

"Okay, I didn't put it quite like that. I gave him a thumbs-up, asked if Livi and the blur were healthy, then suggested we finish cleaning the Ma Deuce. That's a big gun, by the way."

"More equipment?" she murmured before adding, "That's about how I handled it. With a few oohs and aahs thrown in, of course."

"But you didn't see anything?"

"Nope. Just a bunch of wavy lines," she admitted with a sigh. Then she frowned into the dark. "This is why you called me? To ask about Livi and Mitch's sonogram?"

"Nope, that was to break the ice. You know, to bypass your suspicious nature and get you to talk to me."

Tessa had to pry her chin off her chest before she could respond.

"You admit it?"

"Why not. You're smart, you'd have figured it out. This way, I'm honest and upfront, but I'm still on the other side of your defenses."

She wanted to declare it a fail, but, dammit, he was right.

"Aren't you clever," she declared, impressed despite herself.

"Yeah," he said, sounding satisfied. "So what'd you do today?"

And just like that, they slid into the conversation he'd been calling for.

Her earlier unasked question popped into her mind, and before she could stop, it meandered right off Tessa's tongue.

"How long have you been a SEAL?" She waited to be told that was top-secret information.

"Five years with the SEALs, twelve in the Navy," he said easily.

"You joined right out of high school?"

"I joined as soon as I turned eighteen," he clarified. "I wasn't much into school, so I took the GED when I was sixteen."

"Your parents were okay with that?"

"Nobody voiced any objections." His words were smooth and easy, but Tessa could hear the undercurrent there. She wanted to ask questions, to delve deeper. But she knew he'd sidestep her curiosity. After all, that was what she'd do.

"So you didn't have to have a college degree to be a SEAL?" she asked instead, figuring that was safe ground.

"Only to be an officer."

"And that's not something you wanted?"

"More responsibility? Extra work, a higher link in the chain of command?" His laugh was easy, but again, there was a hint of something beneath the surface. "Who needs all that?"

Tessa plucked at the fabric of her blanket, realizing that there was so much more to this man than his sexy looks and charming surface. Suddenly, she wanted to know everything. To ask a million questions that she knew would inspire a million more.

But that wasn't her style. She was all about the surface,

baby. Ignoring the dissatisfaction tapping at her shoulders, she set aside her curiosity.

"So SEALs don't need college degrees," she mused in a lighter tone. "Just a rock-hard body? Or is that something they issue along with your uniform?"

"Body compliments of the US Navy?" He laughed. "Nah. I brought mine from home, but the military definitely put their mark on it. The workouts we do are pretty intense."

"Oh, yeah," she said, remembering the workout video Livi had planned based on the SEAL workout. She'd dropped the project, though, so Tessa had never gone through the exercises. "You guys are the best. I know the basics, but do you actually train every day?"

The conversation easily shifted to fitness, then to the various places their respective careers took them in the name of exercise. It helped to tell herself that she was doing this for her best friend. After all, the better she understood his career, the more supportive she'd be for Livi and Mitch.

But the reality was, Tessa was fascinated.

She lost track of time as she and Romeo talked, their conversation moving from SEAL training to exercise in general when she told him about the months she and Livi had toured with a burlesque troupe, bumping and grinding their way to fitness.

The buzzer by her door rang, letting her know that security had let someone up to see her.

Tessa frowned, wondering who would visit so late.

"Someone's here," she told him, uncurling herself from the couch. "I've got to go."

She was surprised that she actually regretted it.

"It's midnight," he pointed out.

No way. Tessa glanced over her shoulder at the clock on the wall, shocked that they'd talked for so long.

"Do you turn into a pumpkin now?" she asked, peering through the peephole of her front door. Whoever it was apparently hadn't gotten off the elevator yet because she couldn't see anybody.

"No, but creepazoids come calling late at night."

"I thought you said you were on a submarine," she teased.

"I said I spend a lot of time on a submarine."

Her heart skipped a beat. Did that mean he wasn't underwater somewhere? That maybe he was there, on the other side of her door just out of view?

"I'll be fine," she told him. "I live in a secured building, I have a button right next to the door that will call security and I'm a black belt in tae kwon do."

"You're a martial arts expert?" he asked.

"You're surprised?" More than willing to let her impression of him slide back toward the gutter, Tessa didn't challenge him. Instead, she kept her tone neutral. Neutral was the easiest way to let most guys hang themselves.

"Impressed," he said, obviously smarter than most guys. "Want to spar a little next time we see each other?"

"Won't that be the week of the wedding?" she pointed out, hoping he'd correct her. Since he didn't, she added, "I'm thinking wedding week on Catalina is probably not the best time or place for sparring."

"Then we'll have to find something else to do," he promised.

Oh, the many varied and tempting possibilities that filled her mind. All of them were exciting, most of them were better done naked and, oh, so many of them could be easily scheduled between wedding obligations.

She couldn't decide which to suggest first.

The doorbell saved her from having to answer.

"I'm going now," she told him.

She waited for another macho warning, maybe instructions on how she should or shouldn't open the door. Why did men always think they had to do that? she wondered. It was so irritating. As if women didn't have a clue how to watch out for themselves.

"I'll talk to you soon" was all he said, though. Before Tessa could do more than give a surprised blink, he added, "Think about me."

And just like that, he was gone.

She stood there for another second, the phone still pressed to her ear as she tried to process everything that'd happened in the past two hours.

She was pretty sure she'd just had the most interesting conversation with a man she'd ever experienced.

She thought that maybe, possibly, she and Romeo were on the verge of something she'd rarely had with a man—a friendship.

And she was positive that despite their friendly, interesting and completely nonsexual conversation, she was totally turned on.

The only thing she wasn't sure of was when she'd get her hands on the man so she could do something about that.

Then her gaze flew to the door.

A slow smile curved her lips, and she tossed the phone to the couch and hurried across the room.

Her hand on the doorknob, Tessa stopped.

Glancing down at her nightie, she wasn't surprised to see that her nipples were visible, pebbled against the soft cotton. Her toes were bare and she wasn't wearing any panties. Probably not the best attire to greet a visitor.

Then again, she hadn't invited him over.

So if he got all worked up at the sight of her, that was his problem. A problem he'd have to live with since she planned to stick with her no-sex-with-Romeo policy.

Her smile taking on a teasing edge, she shook back her hair, arched her back just enough to thrust out her breasts and then pulled open the door.

He wasn't there.

Nonplussed, she frowned.

She looked to the left, then to the right.

Nobody.

Tessa clenched her teeth against the bitter taste of disappointment. She wanted to blame Romeo, but he hadn't said he was at the door. He hadn't even teased or hinted or led her on in any way.

Nope, that was all her.

Dreaming like a romantic pushover, making up pretty scenarios because she was all gooey over a guy and wanted the fluffy trappings to go with her unfamiliar feelings.

She pulled in a deep breath through her nose, trying to bottle up the scream of frustration that was pounding through her.

A rich, sweet fragrance filled her senses.

Stargazer lilies?

She glanced down.

"Oh," she breathed.

There, knee-high, was an exotic arrangement of purple, red and hot pink spearing out of a triangular glass vase.

Irritation melted into shock before pleasure swept through her. Tessa swore she felt her heart stumble before righting itself.

Unable to resist, she kneeled down to lift the vase, inhaling again the delicious scent. Were they from Romeo? She couldn't see a card in the foliage. Because he'd delivered them in person?

Anticipation dancing through her body like a live wire, she looked around expectantly, sure he'd pop around the corner or stride down the hall at any moment. But thirty seconds passed, then another, and finally, feeling a little stupid, she cupped her arms tight around her flowers and shut the door.

She carried them directly to her bedroom, setting them on her bedside table and checking again for a card or note. But there was nothing to indicate who they were from.

But she knew.

Before she could talk herself out of it, she grabbed the phone and hit Redial. Her smile dimmed when she reached a recorded voice explaining that the number she was trying to reach didn't exist.

Her lower lip in danger of hitting the pouting zone, Tessa slowly set the phone down and focused on the flowers again.

She was sure they were from Romeo. Because hey, clearly covert ops were right up his alley. She breathed in their scent, rubbing one petal of waxy silk between her fingers. The cynical part of her mind—the part that'd ruled most of her twenty-five years—warned that the flowers, like the phone call, were all a part of whatever game he was playing.

He'd thrown down the gauntlet at Livi's engagement party, insisting that he wanted romance before they had sex. This was obviously a part of that romance scheme.

She could be irritated. Maybe she should be. But she wasn't. She couldn't even bring herself to pretend. Instead, Tessa turned off the lights and climbed into bed.

Then she drifted off to sleep with the heady floral scent wrapped around her, a dreamy smile on her face and thoughts of Romeo in her head.

TAPPING HIS CELL phone against his thigh, Gabriel wondered if Tessa liked the flowers. He tried to imagine her face when she opened the door. He knew he'd surprised her, but he wasn't sure what would follow the surprise. Pleasure or cynicism? He wished he were there to watch.

And that, he realized, was the first time he'd ever wished to be somewhere else when he was on duty. It was definitely the first time he'd called a woman from half-way around the world.

And speaking of being halfway around the world, his time was upside down, too. Despite the rising heat of the morning sun, it was time to power down. He looked out over the desolate terrain, absentmindedly cataloging the differences between it and the high desert of the Mojave, where they'd spent the past month conducting nighttime urban-warfare training. This week they'd moved the training halfway around the world.

Given that command had sent them here to train for a week meant that things were quite likely about to get interesting. Gabriel had no concern over interesting assignments. He lived for those.

He was concerned about living through the next one, though, if last night was anything to go by. The men should be operating as a team by now. They'd been assigned together long enough, trained enough, that operations like this should be smooth and seamless. That last night's session had been anything but was an issue.

More specifically, one member was an issue.

Gabriel's shoulder twitched, as if it'd help shake off the nagging irritation that was riding him. He scanned the camp, noting that half the team was still milling about with the support personnel. His gaze landed on Jackrabbit for a long moment before he deliberately turned his back and headed for his tent.

As comfortable in the canvas room as he'd be in a hotel, Gabriel pulled the flap closed and stripped off his shirt. It was clean. He'd put it on after the shower he'd taken before calling Tessa. But it was too damned hot to sleep fully clothed.

He tossed it and the scrambled cell phone onto the small folding table next to his cot.

"Yo, Scavenger," he said to the man on the opposite cot, whose face was buried in a weapons manual. "You ever heard of a *Magic Eye* picture book?"

"Yeah, there's a series of them. Hidden picture books with 3D images made with stereograms." Scavenger squinted at the ceiling. "I think my younger sister used to have a few. Probably still does. You want me to have her ship you one?"

"Thanks. But the last thing your sister shipped me was a box of cinnamon cookies that almost chipped my tooth and a doll stuffed with weeds and wearing a piece of her dress."

Scavenger laughed and set down his book, then rolled on his side and propped himself up on one elbow.

"She'd read that cinnamon was an aphrodisiac, and I think the doll had some sort of love spell on it." Still grinning, Scavenger arched his brows. "You didn't eat any cookies while you were holding that doll, did you?"

"You're kidding, right?" Gabriel had been pursued by some determined women in his life. But none so creative as Scavenger's seventeen-year-old sister. "Those cookies were hard enough to be shot out of an AK-47."

"She's a lousy cook. The doll probably tasted better." Scavenger pulled a face, then shrugged, dismissing his sister as only an older brother could. "So you want a book? I've got other sources if you're worried about what she might hide in the pictures."

Smirking, Gabriel dropped to his bunk to unlace his boots.

"You might want to be worried about a few other things, too," Scavenger suggested.

Gabriel glanced up at the urgency coming through his friend's quiet tone.

"I'm not worried." Before the other man could launch into a lecture, Gabriel shook his head. "Believe me, I'm aware. It'll work out."

"He made deliberate missteps that put you in danger."

Missteps like a throw that fell short by just enough to pull Gabriel off balance, unexplained static over his mic that cut off vital information and taking that building from the north instead of the south, forcing Gabriel to change trajectory at the last second.

"There's no proof that those were deliberate. And the operation was a success."

"There's no guarantee the next one will be, though."

"There's never a guarantee." He took an extra moment to make sure his boots were perfectly aligned under his cot, using the time to beat back the irritation still nagging at him. He didn't know if Jackrabbit had been trying to make him look like an ass last night, or if the guy was trying to do serious damage.

When he straightened, he met Scavenger's angry gaze with a calm look.

"Some teams take longer to build than others. Some trusts are harder to earn." He thought of his call to Tessa. He was pretty sure he'd made a few more vital steps there tonight in earning her trust.

"How long?"

Gabriel shrugged, shucking his fatigues. Not bothering to pull back the blanket, he dropped to the cot wearing just his shorts, hoping the generator-operated cooling unit would keep them from boiling at noon.

"He's not going to stop unless someone makes him," Scavenger said, holding tight to the subject like a dog with a bone. "He can't take the fact that you're better than he is at his own rating, and every other thing. He's totally tweaked over the fact that he's being shown up by an NCO."

"He's pissed because he outranks me but can't outgun me?" Gabriel gave a humorless laugh. "So if I go the OTC route, get my officer training and commission, he'll be okay that I can kick his ass at every single thing?"

"Probably not okay with it. But he'd quit fucking with you."

Crossing his hands behind his head, Gabriel let his mind wander back to Tessa. She was starting to relax with him. He'd never looked for that in a woman before, but it was seriously appealing. Because a relaxed Tessa was an open Tessa.

"What're you going to do about it?"

"Do about what?" Gabriel glanced over to see Scavenger's intense frown.

"Jackrabbit's games."

Nothing that would mess with the team. The team was family; it was everything. But Gabriel wasn't going to say that to Scavenger. Not while the guy was in such an ass-kicking mood.

"I'll watch my ass," he promised instead.

"Fine," Scavenger said, his tone ripe with frustration. "But if he pulls any crap again, you'd better report him."

Closing his eyes as if he were heading for sleep, Gabriel grunted. Hopefully Scavenger would take the sound as agreement. But he wouldn't be reporting anyone. Irish had enough on his plate with the wedding coming up and a baby that looked like a bunch of squiggly lines. The last thing he needed was being stuck refereeing a pissing match.

Gabriel tried to set it all aside and slide into sleep. But it wasn't until he let his mind drift to Tessa, to imagining her face when she'd found her flowers, that he was able to relax.

Crazy, since relaxing was the last thing that ever came to mind when he thought of her.

8

"So GOOD OF you to join us, Tessa."

At Jared's sarcastic welcome, Tessa deliberately slowed her rush into his office to a saunter, but kept her own snarky rejoinder to herself. Just because she was in a vile mood didn't give her reason to take it out on anyone else.

"Sorry I'm running late," she said with a saccharine-sweet smile of her own. She wasn't sure that she wanted to antagonize him. At least, not yet.

She'd actually been here on time, but she had been way-laid by their receptionist-slash-intern, who'd wanted to compliment her on her great shoes, then had whispered the news that she'd overheard Jared calling their accountant for an audit of the books.

She figured she'd see if that little fact came up in the course of the meeting and what the reasoning was. And *then* she'd decide if she wanted to antagonize him.

"Since you're finally here, why don't we get started," Jared said, moving to take his place behind the chrome-and-glass workstation that served as his desk. Or as Maeve liked to call it, his command center. Because he always took command when he sat at it. From his trendy blond hairstyle to his five-hundred-dollar suit to the glossy shine of his shoes, Jared thrived on images. Since Tessa did, too, she knew how important those props were and didn't be-grudge him. At least, not until he tried to use them on her.

It wasn't until Tessa reached the desk that she realized that they weren't the only two people here.

"Hey, Maeve," she said in surprise. Maeve was usually a woman who was difficult to overlook.

"Hey, Tess," Maeve said from where she'd slumped in a chrome-and-leather chair, her head resting on the edge of the backrest and her legs sprawled out in front of her. The redhead's complexion was a delicate shade of green, clashing with her magenta sweatshirt.

"You look like hell," Tessa observed, ignoring Jared's gesture that she take the matching chair so they could begin the meeting. Instead, she dumped her satchel in the chair, then laid the back of her hand on Maeve's forehead. "You're sick. Why are you in here if you're sick?"

"Captain Bligh here commanded my presence."

Tessa turned accusing eyes on Jared.

"You hauled her in here when she's sick? What the hell, Welch? What's so important that this meeting had to be held today?"

And more important, could he justify blowing her chances of seeing Romeo today? With Livi's wedding countdown heading into days now instead of weeks, there was a good possibility that he'd show up soon. She'd never spent this much time thinking about a man as she had Gabriel. She'd never wanted to see one as much as she did him. And Jared's little meeting was delaying that.

She pursed her lips as she looked at her business partner's face. She and Maeve had been trying to nail down what Jared was up to, but for the past two weeks, that'd been a whole lot of nothing. No more questionable behavior; no more suspicious work hours. He'd been back to business as usual. It would have been easy to write her previous misgivings off to an overactive imagination.

Except she knew better.

"I appreciate you both coming in. There are a few things I'd like to discuss."

Tessa glanced at Maeve, feeling better when she saw the other woman had opened her eyes to give him a narrow look.

"Then hurry up and discuss so I can go home," Maeve suggested.

"Of course." And off he went, for the next twenty minutes, outlining where the magazine stood with subscribers, online views and advertising dollars and a couple of marketing angles he wanted input on.

At first, Tessa only listened with half an ear while thinking about Romeo. With the wedding just around the corner, they were guaranteed an entire week in each other's company. A month ago, she'd have figured that was just enough time to seduce him past his silly romance idea, have her wild way with his body a few dozen times and finally get him out of her system.

But now she wasn't so sure she wanted him out of her system. Or that he'd leave even if she tried to boot him. Swinging her leg, she admired the way the light glinted off her patent leather T-straps and mentally pictured herself wearing just the shoes, stockings and Romeo's hands.

Then Jared's words caught her undivided attention.

"We'll need to sideline a few of these new ideas of yours, Tessa. Flirting with life is all well and good, but our focus is on the singles scene. Let's stay focused."

Tessa wanted to growl. She'd worked hard outlining those ideas, making sure each one tied into the singles scene enough to fit their demographic. Jared and Maeve had both agreed that they were a great idea to test out over the next quarter. Tessa figured it was her chance to prove—to herself if nobody else—that she was a solid writer. She gave Jared the evil eye as he continued his spiel. Why was he sidelining her ideas?

"So." He wound up with that big, friendly smile that

always convinced clients to book double their advertising space. "That about sums it up. Are you on board, ladies?"

The only thing she was on board with was the idea of throwing a tantrum over his suggestions. Since all that'd do would be to put Jared's back up, she tried to swallow the string of cuss words clogging her throat.

"Why the changes?" Maeve asked from her slump, not opening her eyes.

"Changes?" His expression as innocent as a Boy Scout, Jared spread his fingers wide as if to ask whatever could she mean. Tessa was sorry Maeve was feeling so lousy, because this really was a great performance that she was missing.

"Changes," Tessa said, finally managing a friendly tone. "Everything you've mentioned today indicates a change in strategy for the magazine from the direction we agreed to earlier this year. Why?"

"Why don't you skip the bullshit and give us the bottom line while you're at it?" Maeve suggested, shifting to sit cross-legged. She planted her elbows on her knees, her chin on her fists, and waited.

Tessa was so relieved she wanted to lean over and kiss the other woman. But she really didn't want whatever bug Maeve was brewing. Instead, she arched one brow at the redhead. Exultation filled her when she got a slight nod in return. It was time to confront Jared and find out what he'd been up to.

"Bottom line?" he asked, his tone dripping with innocence.

"Yes, the bottom line. Explain what you've been sneaking around doing." With a steely look, Tessa added, "While you're at it, you can explain why you called for an audit of our finances, too."

Maeve hissed like a scalded cat, but Tessa kept her eyes

locked on Jared. He looked perfectly at ease, his smile mellow and his eyes calm. But they'd worked together long enough, and she knew men well enough, that she could see the tells. His gaze shifted just a little, focusing on her ear instead of her eyes. He kept rubbing his finger over the edge of his desk, and his pulse was bouncing against his throat like a jackhammer.

"Yes, explain," Maeve said, her nails drumming an angry beat on his desk.

"Okay, well, as you know the magazine is growing at an impressive rate. Impressive enough to catch the eye of some big names. I was approached with an offer."

Tessa's stomach pitched when he named a huge publishing conglomerate. She subscribed to a number of their magazines. Maybe she should be flattered that they wanted the magazine. But without *Flirtatious*, what would she do? What where the odds of finding another job that would hire her to write *sexy* articles about flirting?

Tessa resisted the urge to follow Maeve's lead and press her fingers against her eyelids to stop the pressure pounding there.

"What did they offer?"

He named an amount that made Tessa blink. With that kind of money, she wouldn't have to worry about what to do for at least a year, maybe longer.

"Why didn't you tell us?" she asked faintly.

"In part because it was only an initial offer. It's a good one, but I think we can get more." His eyes wide with studied innocence, Jared lifted his palms. "Before I brought it to the two of you, I wanted to do some research, run a few projections. Based on a few things they'd mentioned and looking into their holdings, I was able to analyze the direction they'll likely take if they buy *Flirtatious*. Once I knew that, I realized that if we initiated the changes and brought in a couple more big advertising accounts, we could ask at least three times what they'd offered."

She tried to process what it all meant. That was obviously a lot of money, but she'd be out of work. She wouldn't have to find new ways to recycle the same topics, but those topics—flirting, the games between the sexes, presenting a pretty picture—were more than just themes. They were who she was.

"The bottom line is that you want to sell *Flirtatious*," Maeve said in a tight voice.

"The bottom line is we have an opportunity to sell it," he countered. "A very lucrative one. We'd be stupid to not consider it."

Her lower lip wanted to tremble, but Tessa held it firm. She knew he hadn't set out to hurt them. She realized that he was only looking out for what was best for the company. But, dammit, she felt as though everything important in her life was slipping away and she couldn't do a thing to stop it.

"What's your plan?" Maeve asked quietly. Her eyes were bloodshot and she seemed a little shell-shocked, but Tessa could see her mind already working.

"First off, we update the format and freshen the look of the magazine, the e-zine and all our social networks. That'd be on you, Maeve. I'll focus on finessing some new advertisers and fine-tuning the proposal."

He gave Tessa a hesitant smile.

"For editorial, the new columns and article slant are vital. The entire magazine revolves around your style, your voice. If you were to begin expanding focus, we'd see the impact much sooner."

"Which means what?" she asked, giving up on saving her makeup—or her eyeballs—and pressing her fingers against her brows to try to relieve the pressure. He wanted her to write articles on flirting with your spouse and date nights for married couples? The Top Ten Pickup Lines to Use While Doing Dishes Together? How was she supposed to do this?

"Which means if you're spearheading the changes, odds are more readers will engage. Then, instead of waiting six months, we could probably go back to the negotiating table in two." Noting the shocked looks on the women's faces, Jared offered a reassuring smile. "Hey, there's no guarantee it'll pan out. If it doesn't, these changes will still make the magazine stronger."

"And if it does?" Tessa asked quietly.

"If it does, and we're all in agreement, we sell the company." He lifted both palms and shrugged. "Then we three go our separate ways, all the richer."

"Go our separate ways…" she repeated on a sigh.

"Nothing lasts forever."

GABRIEL WASN'T A man who believed in judging others.

He'd never ragged on the guys who spent their off hours on the phone with their ladies instead of partying or blowing off steam. He'd never understood it, though.

Until Tessa.

Suddenly he was turning down invites to drive to the nearest base and party at the officers' club because he might catch Tessa before she went to work. He was making excuses to bow out of card games because Tessa should be home from work on her side of the world. He'd even debated giving up sleep one night to call her while she was off work. Except he knew he needed to be fresh and at 100 percent for maneuvers. Especially now that word had come down what they were training for. It was going to be big, and given that Jackrabbit was still being a jackass, Gabriel needed to be on top of his game. As much as he'd like some Tessa time, he couldn't let the team down. He had no problem blowing off bartenders and suckers who wanted to give him their poker money, though.

He watched a few of his teammates and a handful of the support crew head for town, their headlights bright against the desert terrain. Then he vaulted onto the back of one of the cargo trucks, got comfortable and pulled out his cell phone.

It only took two rings before she answered.

"So what're you wearing?"

"Isn't that supposed to be my line?" he asked with a grin, barely noticing as the bands of stress and worry unraveled from his chest.

"Have you ever taken me—or rather, mistaken me—for a traditional kind of woman?"

"Sexy, gorgeous, sweet, clever, savvy, tempting, smart, intriguing, mouthwatering," he recited, imagining her face. A task made easy since he saw it every night in his dreams. "Nope, no *traditional* on my list."

"Well, then?"

Gabriel glanced down at the camouflage pants tucked into heavy boots, the familiar feel of his sidearm nudged against his hip.

"Let's just say I'm dressed for action," he teased.

"Whatever sort of action you're getting, I'll bet what I've got is better," she promised in a tone that sent dual shafts of need straight through his body. Since sex was as vital to his well-being as air, he was pretty familiar with the physical need. But the emotional need? He'd never felt that before.

Which made her even more dangerous than the action he was seeing here on maneuvers, he realized. He just wasn't sure how he wanted to deal with that fact. Avoid, engage or eliminate?

"What'd you come up with for your fifth spring break pickup line?" he asked, figuring it smarter to change the subject than to worry about all that crazy thinking right now.

"'I forgot my number, can I have yours?'" she said in a deep voice, ending with a laugh.

"Seriously? Something that cheesy would work?"

"Not on me, but it's all about the audience," she reminded him. "Spring break usually means drunk coeds and wet T-shirt contests. Cute and cheesy go hand in hand."

She paused, and he could easily imagine she was scrunching her brows together as she shook her head, her long hair sliding over that silken skin. His body, already stirring at the sound of her voice, hardened more.

"How can you be so hot and not know these things?" she asked. "I can't believe you are so seriously bad at pickup lines."

He grinned at the memory of their brainstorming session a few nights ago. She'd rejected every one he'd come up with, finally suggesting that he ask the team for theirs instead.

"I told you once, I've told you a hundred times. I don't need pickup lines."

"Right. Because the women throw themselves at you," she teased. "Poor guy, I'll bet you can't even have a nice, quiet night out with the boys without having to climb over the prostrate bodies of your worshippers."

"It's a rough life," he agreed. "As I'm sure you know, seeing as you can't have a nice, quiet night out with the girls without having to fend off your own worshippers spouting lousy pickup lines."

"If they read my next column, they'll have some amazing pickup lines," she pointed out. "No thanks to you, of course."

"Hey, now," he protested halfheartedly.

Her laugh was pure delight, filling him with a weird sort of feeling, like a warm glow in his chest.

"How goes countdown: wedding?" he asked, not really caring but not willing to analyze that weird feeling. He'd taken a few hits to the chest that morning. He'd write it off to internal injuries.

"Oh, you know, a change here, a change there," she said, the smooth words not quite disguising the hurt and frustration he could hear beneath. "I guess Livi found a different dress, so the ceremony will be a little more formal to accommodate it."

More formal? Gabriel could feel the imaginary tie choking him.

"What happened to that perfect dress the two of you spent weeks finding?" he asked, remembering her tales of traveling from store to store, town to town, with Livi. That was pretty much the most excited he'd heard her in any discussion about the wedding.

"Oh, boy. Pauline found some table scheme she liked better and wanted to change around a few things. By the time she was done, nothing was the same."

Gabriel had never understood the whole wedding hoopla. A party was a party, wasn't it?

He'd take a life-or-death mission over planning a wedding any day. And from the sound of it, Tessa probably would, too. If nothing else, he knew he should be grateful that no matter how bizarre, overwhelming and unexpected his feelings for her were, she was as antimarriage as he was. It was like having a fail-safe built into their relationship.

Gabriel blinked at the pitch-black night, his frown sliding into a scowl.

Were they actually in a relationship?

How the hell had that happened?

Maybe he should have stuck with his usual MO. Dive right into great sex, revel in the pleasures, then move on.

But instead, he'd outsmarted himself. He'd been so focused on getting Tessa hooked, on making her want more than just great sex, that he'd somehow hooked himself, too.

Sliding into battle mode, his mind raced as he considered the options and angles. Emotional trajectory was a different field for him, but he didn't figure it could be any more hazardous than targeting explosives. All he had to do was shift his aim by a careful margin and he'd be back on track, avoid the emotional tangles and still achieve his target of incredible sex.

With that in mind, Gabriel slid down a little lower against the back of the truck, let his head fall to rest on the cool metal and closed his eyes.

"Poor baby," he murmured. "It sounds as though you need something to take your mind off all that wedding drama. If I were there, I'd take care of that for you."

"Would you, now?" she purred, easily falling in with the sexy talk.

"I'd start with a massage," he decided. "Hot oil, hard hands, your bare skin. My fingers are magic, you know. They'll find the perfect spot to drive all thought out of your mind, the perfect pressure to send your body into a melting puddle of pleasure."

"Mmm," she breathed. "I can't wait."

"Just a few more days," he said, the husky growl a promise to them both. A few more days and, somewhere between all the wild sexual positions he planned to explore with her body, he'd find time for a massage. "In the meantime, why don't you hit the spa there at the hotel? Loosen up a little so you're not so stressed."

Not that he had any doubts about his ability to get her

off in record time, stress or no stress. But he didn't like the idea of her being all tensed up until he could take care of her.

"I'm not in Catalina yet. I was called in for an emergency meeting at *Flirtatious* yesterday that's had me tied up at home."

His smile fell away at the edge in her voice, the easy sexual buzz bursting as concern took its place.

"Did you figure out what's going on with your partner?" he asked. A partner Gabriel planned to meet and assess for himself as soon as he was back on base. The guy sounded like a cross between a boy-band wannabe and a used-car salesman. Gabriel had no doubt that Tessa could handle the guy, but he'd still like to get a look for himself.

"I have a pretty good idea what's up," she said in a worried tone. Then she cleared her throat and added brightly, "But that's boring. Work drama is no more fun than wedding drama. I'd much rather talk about something sexier... like the fact that you never did tell me what you're wearing."

Her voice dropped to a seductive pitch, but there was a chilly edge to it that told Gabriel just how upset she was. Tessa used her sexuality as a shield, throwing it out there to push people away.

He understood. A part of him wanted to push her, to accuse her of closing him out, using charm and flirtations to distract him while hiding her true self. Except he'd been on the receiving end of that accusation enough to know how irritating it was to hear, even if it were true.

Besides, he'd decided only minutes ago that this was all about sex. So why did he care that she was making sure it stayed there? He clenched and unclenched his fist, imagining himself crushing the frustration that surged at that choice. Didn't matter. Neither of them were relationship material, so they should focus on what they were best at.

Pleasure.

"All I'm wearing is a towel," he said. "It's knotted at my waist, but I'll bet nimble fingers could untie it pretty fast."

"I'll bet a clever mouth could get it off even faster. My fingers would be busy exploring what's beneath it. I'd slide them up your thighs, maybe skim one hand around to see if your ass is as tight and sweet bare as it is in those jeans you wear."

"As tight and sweet as the hot temptation between your thighs?" he asked, easily sliding into sexy talk while ignoring the chiding voice in the back of his head warning that he was just fooling himself by thinking he could contain something this powerful.

"If you touch me, you'd know that I'm not only tight and sweet, I'm wet and waiting," she said, her quickening breath audible over the phone. "After I nip that knot open and let the towel fall to the floor, I'd let you touch me. Just one finger, though, and only for a moment. Long enough for you to see how wet I am, to taste my juices."

"Do you really think I'd stop at one moment once I touch you?"

"You'd have to," she promised. "Because as soon as you taste, I'll move. I'll shift to my knees again and slide my lips over your rock-hard shaft. I'll lick you like a lollipop, nibbling and tasting every long, throbbing inch."

Gabriel's own breath was coming faster now. His dick was rivaling concrete beneath his zipper, blood pounding through it like a drumbeat.

"You're killing me," he admitted with a groan. "You have no idea how hard this is."

"I'll bet I could make it harder if I could really touch you," she said with a husky laugh.

"Believe me, I'm more than ready to be touched," he said. He was pretty sure he'd hit a new record for days with an unrelieved hard-on. It was a small camp, too small for enough privacy to relieve the intense sexual pressure he'd been sporting since he'd started this little game with Tessa.

"A couple of days," she promised.

He almost threw his phone across the desert when it buzzed, signaling that he'd reached the call limit. His body screaming protests, he clenched his teeth, angled himself upright and took a deep breath.

"I've gotta go," he said, unable to disguise the frustration in his tone.

"Aww, and just when things were getting good." Instead of frustration, Tessa's voice was filled with laughter. Not exactly ego boosting, but he was glad the stress and tension from earlier was gone.

"Sucks, but I've hit my transmission limit," he said, glancing at the phone to see he only had seconds left. "I guess nothing lasts forever."

Her quick intake of breath was sharp and painful, making him frown through the sexual haze.

"Be safe" was all she said, though. Then the phone went dead. That was it. No recriminations, no begging for assurances he couldn't offer.

Damned if she wasn't amazing.

His forearms resting on his updrawn knees, Gabriel stared out into the desert, the pitch-black canvas offering no distraction as he imagined Tessa's face. He'd planned this with the same care and precision he'd plan a mission. He'd figured romance was just a fancy way to package up sexual foreplay. Another type of game that'd give him the upper hand in this ongoing challenge with a woman he hadn't figured out yet. No big deal, right?

Define your path, stand your ground and never let any-

one else's actions define your own. The basis for every one of his other life rules. Like the one about going it alone as long as he served in the Navy.

He'd defined the path with Tessa by insisting they have a romance, and as hard as it'd been—he shifted uncomfortably at the pun—he'd stood his ground. But her actions, her reactions, the simple sweetness he'd discovered beneath the sexy exterior… All of that had him considering some serious redefining.

He dropped his forehead to his knees, replaying the ricocheting slew of emotions that'd rammed through his system in that seven-minute phone call. He'd never felt these things before. He blew out a breath. Maybe it was time to consider rethinking a few of those rules. Like the one about going it alone…

"Petty Officer Thorne, you got a minute?"

9

GABRIEL JUMPED DOWN from the truck bed, a frown curving his mouth. He cast a quick glance around, but nobody else was there but Irish. Since when did Donovan refer to him by his rank when they were alone?

"Sir," he responded, automatically coming to attention.

"We need to discuss the incident that took place on the field today."

"Incident?" Gabriel's gut clenched but his blank expression didn't change. Irish hadn't been on the field today. He'd been at headquarters being briefed on the training changes and mission details.

"Oh-eleven-twenty-three, equipment malfunction that resulted in a blow to your chest, sending you flying across the back of a Humvee into a building, the resulting collision possibly offering warning to the natives that unfriendlies were in the area. You made up the loss of those approximate three minutes by scrambling, still managing to detonate the explosive on schedule, hence allowing the rest of the team to complete their mission unencumbered by said incident."

That clenching in Gabriel's gut tightened to a vicious knot, both at the recital and at the officiously cold stance it was offered in. Then the knot twisted painfully as he realized how Irish must have got his information.

Scavenger? He knew Shane was pissed over Jackrabbit's games, but he'd never have imagined the guy doing an end run around his order to let it go. So who? Mr. Wizard? Bad Ass? Auntie?

Gabriel's belly burned with the embers of betrayal.

"Who's the rat?"

Irish's expression barely changed. A slight shift of his brow, his lips tightened and his shoulder twitched maybe a millimeter.

And just like that, chastisement.

Gabriel gritted his teeth, realizing that was one of the things that made Irish such a stellar leader. The man knew how to push buttons with just a look. Now instead of being righteously indignant at being ratted on like a schoolboy, he felt like a total jerk for questioning the motivation of his teammates.

"Lieutenant Banks is leading this operation," Irish informed him in that same official tone. "He wrote the book on protocol and follows it to the letter. So much so that he's been known to lead a mission one man short when one of his team sustained a minor injury."

Still smarting at the unspoken reprimand, Gabriel shrugged.

"Didn't that prove to be a mistake?" he asked, since that particular mission had resulted in Banks being captured.

"Trusting the wrong person proved to be the mistake."

Shit. Gabriel closed his eyes, rocking back on his heels for just a moment while he tried to shake off the feeling of being an absolute dick. He wasn't privy to the details of that mission, but he'd caught enough rumors to know that Banks had tried to warn command of the potential mole but intelligence had ordered him to proceed as planned.

"Acknowledged," Gabriel murmured, opening his eyes and nodding to show he was in the wrong.

"Banks will watch the same video that I did as he works through the plan, assessing the team's strengths and weaknesses." Irish paused, letting that sink in long enough for Gabriel to nod his acceptance of the slap down and the feeling of being a complete ass over the accusation settle. Then he continued, "And he's going to see one very specific weakness that he'd be smart to eliminate."

"Jackrabbit?" Gabriel seriously hated thinking badly about a teammate, and even worse hated the idea that he couldn't find a way to work with every member of his team. But dammit, he'd be glad to see that whining jerk finally get what was coming to him.

"You."

If Irish had pulled out his pistol and slapped him upside the head with it before dancing a jig over his prone body while singing show tunes, Gabriel couldn't have been more shocked.

Or horrified.

"Me?" he repeated, hoping he'd heard wrong.

"You." Irish gave a barely perceptible arch of one brow, waiting for the implication to sink in.

And it did, like a lead weight. Painfully slow, ruthlessly undisputable. His commanding officer, his team leader, his best friend considered him a weakness.

He'd rather be pistol-whipped to show tunes.

Knowing Irish wouldn't continue until that point had been recognized, Gabriel gave a jerk of his chin. His lips pressed tight, he was starting to feel like a bobblehead with all this nodding to acknowledge his mistakes.

"From your expression, and your response, I'm going to assess that this isn't the first incident," Irish said, lifting one hand to stave off any response. "Which means it's an ongoing hostile situation. Knowing you as I do, I'm going to further assess that you've already taken every means possible to peaceably deal with it."

"I've considered a few nonpeaceable means," Gabriel

admitted under his breath. Hell, in the past two minutes he'd imagined at least a dozen more that were leaning quite close to straight-up violence.

"Given these circumstances, and the fact that Banks will be on-site at first light, I'm going to give you one last chance to rectify the situation before I take steps myself."

Steps.

Gabriel scowled. A part of him wanted to ask exactly what those steps might be, but he knew there was a fine line between Irish's friendship with him and his stance as his commanding officer. To ask was to risk insubordination.

Still...

"You'd pull me from the team?" Gabriel challenged—which wasn't exactly the same as asking.

"I'd recommend that you be pulled from this mission. Where it went from there would be out of my hands." Irish tilted his head to one side. "And that'd be a crappy position to put me in, wouldn't it?"

Guys had been pulled from missions for injury before, every once in a while because of scheduling conflicts. But to be pulled for endangering the mission, which was how this would go down? Yeah. He'd be off the team.

Fury the likes of which he'd rarely felt pounded through his system. The SEAL team was his life. Being a part of it, it was who he was. He'd been fine waiting for Jackrabbit to pull his head out of his ass and realize he couldn't win. Hell, waiting the guy out had become something of a challenge in itself. One Gabriel had been willing to take to the limits to win.

His rage was so intense, he couldn't tell whether he was angrier at Jackrabbit for putting him in this mess, or at the fact that he was forcing Gabriel to concede the win in order to get out of the mess.

It didn't matter. Fists clenched, Gabriel called on the training of his youth to channel every ounce of that anger into his hands, squeezing it tight until it he'd released it completely.

A deep breath through his teeth cleared away the last dregs of emotion, leaving behind a pool of calm.

"I didn't intend to put you, or the team, in a bad position," he admitted quietly, letting the tension pour out of his shoulders as he leaned against the truck to gesture to the camp. "I just figured it'd blow over, you know. The Navy doesn't let idiots into the SEALs. The guy had to clue in sooner or later."

"Some guys have an issue with second place," Irish acknowledged. "That doesn't make him an idiot."

Gabriel grunted his annoyance.

"The lengths he went to do it, though," Irish muttered, making Gabriel's lips twitch.

"Why the hell didn't you tell me?" Irish asked, scowling as he slipped out of his role as commanding officer to simply be a friend. He relaxed enough to lean one hip against the truck and shake his head. "The guy really is a complete dumb ass. You know I'd have had your back."

"You've got enough on your plate." Gabriel shrugged. "This promotion to head up the training programs, a baby on the way, your upcoming wedding. Last thing you need is to be brought up on charges of assaulting a dumb ass."

After a long stare, Irish gave a slow, pitying shake of his head.

"You're so busy protecting the team, protecting me, that you aren't covering your own ass. I get that brotherhood is priority, believe me. But you're taking loyalty too far. You're letting it make you a victim."

"The hell I am," Gabriel snapped, the anger returning with a vengeance as he shoved forward with clenched fists, this time ready for battle. He'd never been a victim. He'd made damned sure of that and nobody, not even his best friend, was going to say otherwise.

"No?" Irish gave him a cool look, obviously not intimidated by Gabriel's threatening stance. "You're playing fair, working for the good of the team. Meanwhile, this asshole is so busy trying to prove you're not invincible that he's going to get you seriously hurt in training. Or worse, killed in action."

Gabriel's fury drained, leaving him cold. And a little dizzy at the unfamiliar barrage of emotions hitting him tonight.

"You should have reported Jeglinski when this started," Irish said quietly. "There are channels in place for dealing with exactly this sort of dispute."

"That's not my way." Gabriel shook his head. The military equivalent of tattling. "I'm sure there are alternatives."

"Cut the stoic crap," Irish snapped with a frustrated glare. "There's a big difference between tolerating rough conditions to accomplish the objective and letting an unnecessary complication fuck up your career."

Gabriel grinned, amused as always to hear Irish swear like that. He stood by his statement. He wasn't a victim. But if this kept up, someone else might be.

And hell, he'd been considering rethinking his rules to build a relationship with Tessa. It made more sense to rethink them to save his relationship with his team. And yeah, his career.

"Fine. I'll deal with it."

"You'll file a complaint?" When Gabriel jerked his chin in the affirmative, Mitch gestured toward his quarters. "Good, let's go."

"Not to you. I'm not bringing you into this. If there's a strike, it's going on my record and mine alone." Gabriel cast an assessing eye over the camp, knowing nobody had heard a word they said, yet the entire platoon would have all the details within hours. "Jackrabbit isn't going to roll over and accept the charges. He'll fight and he'll fight dirty."

Gabriel didn't need to explain that whatever measures Irish took with the complaint, Jeglinski would find a way to construe it as favoritism. Gabriel's own refusal to speak out about the other man's actions before would play into his hands, too. Only a bright-eyed optimist would think this was going to go down any way but ugly.

And while Gabriel might be called many things—charming, clever, lucky, talented, among others—he'd never, ever been deemed an optimist.

Mitch shook his head, exasperation glinting in his eyes. "Seriously, dude. You don't have to protect everyone."

"Nope. Not everyone," Gabriel agreed. "Just everyone who matters."

NOTHING LASTS FOREVER.

The eerie way Romeo's words had echoed Jared's was still nagging at Tessa several days later as the helicopter approached Catalina.

It wasn't as if she wanted forever.

But if her whole world was going to turn upside down, she'd like to be the one choosing to change it. Or at least doing wildly outrageous, completely indulgent things that resulted in the changes. That would fit her reputation so much better than this mess.

It wasn't just her friendship with Livi or her career that was changing, either. Even the…whatever it was she had with Romeo was a major change for her. But as incredibly sexy as he was, as mind-blowingly intriguing as she d him and how surprisingly sweet he'd proved to be, all she'd been interested in was sex. But no, he'd wanted romance. And somehow his insistence on romance had turned into this…whatever it was they had between them.

Tessa stared out the bubble-shaped window at the ocean beyond, the water rough and choppy and tipped in white.

Now her life felt like that ocean, and this…whatever between them was the only thing keeping her from drowning. When she talked to Romeo, all the stress fell away. The worries and doubts and feeling of being adrift without having a clue who she was all faded.

He made her smile. Real, from-the-heart smiles that took a while to fade.

He made her laugh. At his silly jokes, at life in general, even at herself.

He made her think. About choices, about life. About them.

And, oh, baby, he made her hot. All she had to do was close her eyes and imagine his smile and her thighs would tremble. If she imagined his hands, too, she'd get wet. His voice was pure seduction, and when he started talking dirty…

Realizing she was trembling, Tessa shook her head as if that'd help erase the thoughts lodged there. It didn't matter, though. Because Romeo wasn't leaving.

She held her breath, her stomach diving into her toes, and not just because the helicopter was landing.

How was it possible that he'd become so important that she felt as though she needed him—not wanted, but really needed him—yet she hadn't even seen him naked? She hadn't felt his body slide over hers, welcomed his hard length inside her. She didn't know if he liked it fast or slow. She could only imagine what his face looked like when he came.

But that was what this weekend was for.

To touch him. To feel him. To revel in the perfection of his body. She took a shaky breath, her mouth watering as she imagined how he'd taste. Oh, his taste. She was going to start at the sharp angle of those gorgeous cheek-bones and nibble her way to his mouth. After spending a few minutes—hours, weeks—kissing, she'd lick her way over that chest, down his flat belly and then she'd get to the good stuff.

The thud of the helicopter setting down burst her fan-tasy. Thankful for the pilot's helping hand, Tessa climbed out of the helicopter on shaking legs.

"You're here!" Livi declared and rushed forward to wrap her arms around Tessa so tightly that Tessa almost fell over.

"Hey." With one hand trying to keep her hair from whipping her in the face, she patted Livi on the back with the other, a little worried that she'd either fly away or be squeezed to bits. "Are you okay?"

"Sure. Fine. Great."

Uh-huh. Sure she was.

Despite the very strong, very fit arms wrapped around her, Tessa managed a deep breath and ushered the pair of them a little farther away from the helicopter and its wind-whipping blades.

"Why don't we get a drink and you can fill me in on all the greatness," Tessa said. Livi nodded, but she didn't let go. "Or, you know, we can just stay here for a while."

Livi gave a sniffling sort of laugh, but finally un-wrapped herself.

"Sorry. I think I'm a just a little overwhelmed."

"With all the greatness?" Tessa said, keeping the sar-casm to a minimum when she saw the stress etching lines on Livi's face. She didn't know a lot about happy-ever-after, but she was pretty sure a bride wasn't supposed to be sporting worry-induced wrinkles the week before the wedding.

"Do you remember when the *Fit To Be Naked* workout series hit so big?" When Tessa nodded, Livi pushed her hair off her face and sighed. "It was a huge success, right? Everything I'd worked so hard for and really wanted, boom. Done."

"But you were miserable," Tessa responded quietly.

"Crazy, right?"

Before Tessa could say no, the driver gestured that he'd loaded her luggage in the car and was ready to go. Livi ushered her into the vehicle, telling the driver where to take them, then settled back in the seat.

"It's nothing," Livi said, her smile bright again. "I'm just nervous. It's been like this all week. Ups, downs. If my mood could go sideways I'm sure it would. It's probably hormones."

Hormones, her ass. Tessa knew that Livi was always up when she was doing things the way she wanted and down when others shoved their opinions and agendas down her throat—usually saying they were for her own good.

But reminding her of that wasn't going to help the situation.

"That or the idea of going without sex for the past couple of weeks before the wedding," Tessa said with a wicked arch of her brow, as always falling back on naughty when she didn't know what to do. "A hottie on hand and no sex would drive me sideways, for sure."

Livi gave a relieved laugh, her smile a little too bright again as she gripped Tessa's hand.

"I'm so glad you're here," she said fervently. "Everything is changing so fast, so much is going on. I always feel braver dealing with that sort of thing with you at my side."

Tessa blinked away tears, her fingers entwining with

Livi's. Even as her friend's engagement ring cut into her skin, she could actually feel the protective layer of ice she'd built around her heart melting a little.

"I wish you could have the perfect wedding," Tessa said quietly. "Your dream wedding."

"Well, I have my dream man, which is what really counts," Livi said, her gaze shifting to the window to watch the pretty scenery flash by. "And I'm really glad we're getting married here on Catalina, even if it's a little fancier than I'd hoped. But maybe we'll come back and renew our vows in five or ten years with that cliff-side ceremony I'd originally wanted. Just me and Mitch, with you and Gabriel as our witnesses."

Gabriel.

Delightful little tingles of pleasure swirled through her system just hearing his name. She took a second to revel in the familiarity of lust, sliding easily into the one thing she still understood, still felt comfortable with.

She held tight to that lust, letting the passion she felt for Gabriel become her anchor in the craziness that was every single other thing in her life.

"What do you think?" Livi asked, clearly oblivious to her little interlude. "Won't it be fun?"

"Cozy," Tessa agreed. This time she was the one who had to put the extra wattage in her smile.

Five years from now she was pretty sure the only place she'd have in Gabriel's life was a notation in the little black book he kept in his head.

And in Livi's? She bit her lip. Well, she was working on that, wasn't she? All she had to do was get through this wedding with her agreeable facade in place, and odds were that she'd be around for a while.

"So is everything set for the wedding week?" she asked.

As Livi launched into her description of the weeklong

entertainment plans, then on to changes in the ceremony, all Tessa could think was thank God Pauline wasn't a fan of YouTube or trendy wedding crazes. Because there was no way in hell she was body popping her way down the aisle in a strapless dress.

"My dress is still the strapless chiffon in purple, isn't it?" she asked with a slight frown. "The one I had the final fitting for last week?"

Her jaw clenched. The only one she'd loved out of the thirty-seven she'd had to try on for Pauline's approval.

"Oh, yeah, your dress is the same," Livi said, a stubborn look coming into her eyes. "Pauline thought the color might be too strong and wanted to get a pale peach shade instead but I said no."

Imagining the damage pale peach would do to her skin tone, Tessa gave a slight shudder. She gripped Livi's hand in gratitude, knowing it couldn't have been easy for her to stand up to Pauline.

It only took a few minutes to get from the helipad to the luxury beachside hotel, but it was enough time to get an eyeful of Catalina. Mostly because it wasn't a very big island. It was gorgeous, though. Small and picturesque, surrounded by the dramatic power of the ocean, it practically screamed romance.

She said as much when Livi finally paused to take a breath.

"It is gorgeous, isn't it?" Livi agreed, staring out the window. "I fell in love with it when Mitch brought me here for the weekend. The cliffs are amazing. Dramatic and powerful, with this feeling of endurance."

"What changed your mind about having the ceremony there?"

"It really wasn't practical to ask guests to climb cliffs in formalwear, and the wind would probably make a mess of my hair." Livi shrugged, the dreamy look on her face falling away. Tessa wanted to scream at her to put it back, dammit.

Instead, she took a deep breath and bit her lip, then, unable to keep her mouth shut, leaned forward.

"You know, you've filmed exercise workouts on a cliff without your hair being an issue, and I can't imagine any guest bitching about the locale considering everything you're doing to entertain them this week." And if they did, Tessa was more than ready to take them aside for a little chat. "This is supposed to be your day, your dream. Why aren't you doing it your way?"

"I did it my way at my first wedding, remember? And it was a disaster, right down to the wrong flowers, the rain and that horrible whole-grain cake. My mother didn't talk to me for months afterward. And after all of that, it still ended in divorce a few years later." Livi's face fell, the pain of everything she'd gone through clear in her eyes. "I know it's silly and superstitious, but this time I'm not taking any chances. This time, instead of pretending I can handle it, I'm letting the experts take over."

There had to be a middle ground that would still let Livi have her dream wedding, but Tessa figured that since her particular expertise was actually pretending she could handle things, she'd just keep her mouth shut. Besides, the unfortunate memory of that cake was still clear in her mind. If nothing else, she could be grateful that there would be no soy buttercream or oatmeal cakes this week.

"But hey, if we can't have the drama and excitement of the cliffs, this is a great venue," Livi said with a smile, her expression hopeful as they pulled up to the hotel. "Pauline was worried the ballroom wouldn't be elegant enough, but once she changed a few things she decided it would work."

Elegant enough? Tessa sighed. She appreciated pomp

and drama. Hell, she lived for it. But Livi was more suited to fairy-tale romance than chic sophistication. Deciding to give it one last try, she waited until they were out of the car.

"As long as you and Mitch are happy," Tessa said.

Livi's face softened at the mention of her fiancé. Maybe that was the key, Tessa realized with a frown. Livi was so hung up on the guy that he was her dream. The actual wedding, with its elaborate plans and carefully staged pomp, was just one day. Her brow twitching, Tessa amended that to one very stressful, extremely expensive day.

"Mitch is amazing," Livi said, gesturing for Tessa to precede her into the hotel lobby. It was like walking into an underwater grotto with its rich shades of blue and purple, twisted glass in the corner and glistening lights dangling overhead.

This, at least, suited Livi.

Tessa checked in while Livi extoled the many and varied virtues of one Mitch Donovan. Since all of those virtues seemed to have a PG rating, Tessa only listened with half an ear. Even half an ear was enough to make her nervous, though.

She could understand the temptation to lose yourself in a certain kind of man. A sexy man with a clever mouth and an intriguing mind. One who laughed easily, who understood the little games between the sexes and didn't get all weird about them. One with dark eyes and black hair, razor-sharp cheekbones and lips that could melt a girl in two seconds flat. What else could a man like that do? she wondered. Once he got going, he could probably do absolutely anything. And do it very, very well.

She wet her lips, her breath a little tight at the idea of just what Gabriel could do. She'd had more orgasms with the man by telephone than she'd had in most of her so-called relationships. Needing to cool off a little, she slipped her sweater off to let the air waft over her bare shoulders.

He was quickly becoming the only stable thing in her life. It was as if he were her touchstone to something she understood.

Sex.

The kind of sex she could become addicted to.

And that was the problem with losing yourself in someone, she realized. How did you find yourself again when it was over? So tired of struggling with her own identity crisis, Tessa shuddered. What if there was simply nothing left?

"I'm hoping Mitch will be here in the next day or so."

Livi's words cut through Tessa's frantic head trip. Taking her old-fashioned key from the concierge, she turned to Livi with a frown.

"Mitch isn't here yet?"

"He's on duty," Livi said simply.

On duty? This was their wedding week. Wasn't he supposed to be here, participating or something? Tessa couldn't imagine herself ever getting married, but if she did, she'd damned well expect her husband-to-be right there, suffering beside her.

Wasn't Livi pissed? She narrowed her eyes, inspecting her friend's face. All she saw was a calm glow. It was freaky.

"How do you do that?" Tessa asked, marveling. "I mean, I've seen you take on a lot of pretty intense challenges, but I'm blown away at how you've adapted to this military thing. I can't imagine being so at peace with it all."

"It's who Mitch is. Asking him to change that would be like his asking me to give up exercise. Since fitness is my career, my lifestyle and my passion, giving it up would change who I am."

Tessa bit her lip but couldn't stop herself, and asked, "But don't you worry?"

"Would it help if I did?" Livi mused, staring out the wall of windows at the ocean. "Maybe it's the years I spent letting other people run my business and direct my life. But I just don't see how worrying is productive. It'd stress me out, it'd upset Mitch and it wouldn't make any difference at all to whatever outcome I was worrying about."

Having seen some of the disasters other people had created in Livi's life, Tessa was truly baffled at the idea of simply letting things happen.

"But isn't worrying about something the first step to changing it for the better?" she asked.

"Has worrying about *Flirtatious* helped you fix the issues there?" Livi asked with a gentle smile.

Tessa wanted to growl. This peaceful Zen pregnancy thing Livi had going on was going to drive her crazy. Especially since she had a point.

"You know Jared is up to something. You're doing everything in your power to figure it out. And since you're a strong, smart woman, you also know that whatever happens, you'll be okay." Livi arched her brows. "Right?"

"Ri-i-ight," Tessa said, her reluctance drawing the word out into three syllables. She debated filling Livi in on the details of what was actually going on. But as she had every time she considered it over the past few days, she immediately tucked the thought away. Livi didn't need to hear her problems right now. Not with everything else she had going on.

Besides, if she told her, Livi would ask how Tessa felt about it, what she wanted. And she simply didn't know. It was bad enough feeling confused and lost without admitting it.

"Then, what good is it to worry? How's that going to

help?" Livi asked in a tone so reasonable that all Tessa could do was offer a stiff smile.

"So, no Mitch," she said instead. "Knowing Pauline, his list of assignments was at least as long as mine. Is there anything I can do to help cover until he gets here?"

Livi smiled, tucking her arm into Tessa's as a young man approached them with a tray.

"Like any good groom, Mitch sent his second-in-command. Gabriel got in yesterday. He's such a sweetie. He's been helping with everything, including keeping Pauline off my back." Livi pressed her tongue to her upper lip before grinning. "Well, everything except that satisfaction part."

"Oh, but he'd be so good at it," she teased. "Isn't that how he built his reputation? On charm, that wicked smile and a slew of satisfied smiles?"

"More than a slew, if this week is anything to go by." Livi laughed. "Poor Gabriel. Everywhere we go there are women throwing themselves at him."

Really...

A vicious buzzing filled her ears.

She wanted to ask if he'd caught any of them. But Tessa—the queen of sexual freedom and no strings— couldn't bring herself to say those words because the image of Romeo with anyone filled her with blinding fury. She'd never been a possessive woman—with the notable exceptions of her shoes and her friendship with Livi—nor did she feel an ounce of jealousy over the myriad of women in Romeo's past. But his present? His future?

Her stomach clenched.

She'd just have to seduce him stupid and make sure he was too sexually spent to get even a hint of a rise for any of those other women. She'd give him the best sex of his life, hook him as if he was an addict and she the only dealer in his world.

Romeo wouldn't know what hit him. Because she'd be damned if anyone else was getting a piece of that man until she'd had her fill.

And given the way she was feeling, she might never be full.

"Would you be interested in a drink to welcome you to Casa Bella, ladies?" the waiter offered, his voice breaking through Tessa's bizarre trip into emotional overload.

With a murmured thanks, Livi accepted an iced sparkling juice. Still reeling at her reaction to imagining Gabriel with someone else, Tessa had to blink a couple of times before she could focus on the tray.

"Tequila?" Tessa asked, eyeing the tall glass of what looked like a melting sunset. At his nod, she grabbed it with unladylike haste. And gave a momentary thanks that Livi had hold of one arm, otherwise she'd probably have grabbed two.

Before she could swallow a sip of the soothing alcohol she felt a tingle. Like the gentle fingers of the sun skimming over her body—barely there but very discernible. A knot tightened in her belly—whether it was nerves or sexual need, she didn't know.

"Oh, there's Gabriel now."

She didn't need her friend's delighted exclamation to tell her what her body was already screaming out. Livi turned to wave. Since her arm was still linked through Tessa's, Tessa turned, too.

And froze. Which was the only reason her smile didn't fall clean away.

Romeo.

Casual in jeans and a black T-shirt that hugged his broad shoulders and lovingly skimmed those mouthwatering biceps, his grin lit up the room. His eyes were locked on Tessa's, making it impossible for her to look away.

Trapped by that dark gaze, her mind spun in a million directions, even as her body heated, passion engaging instantly. Her nipples poked against the satin of her bra in a desperate greeting, her stomach tight with excitement.

She'd have ignored it all if she could.

But all she could do was wet her lips and stare.

Well, well. There he was, her lust anchor.

Tessa might not know how to tell her best friend that she had backslid into being a complete doormat, or have any idea how to express her frustration over being totally shoved aside. She might not have a clue what to do about her own future or how to keep her career from imploding.

But this feeling she had for Romeo?

The edgy lust that tangled tight with sweet passion's promise?

She knew *exactly* what to do with that.

10

GABRIEL STOPPED SHORT just inside the balcony doors, his ears ringing as if he'd had a close call with a cluster bomb. His senses hit full alert, muscles tight and brain racing to assess the possible damage.

As a man who specialized in blowing things up, he'd know danger when he saw it. And the woman standing not twenty feet away was pure danger, for a multitude of reasons.

Not the least of which was that she was so damned gorgeous.

Gabriel's gaze heated as he looked her over. Long black hair streamed like a waterfall over her bare shoulders, almost hiding the tiny red straps of her little red dress. The fabric curved like a temptation over her ample breasts, then tapered along her waist before flaring gently over her hips to flow to her knees. There was nothing provocative about her look—if anything it was simple and sedate compared to Tessa's usual sensual style.

Now his body was rock hard for a very different reason. His ears ringing with the sounds of Tessa's orgasms as they'd echoed through his cell phone. Heat funneled through his system, loosening his muscles even as his fingers flexed in preparation for the delightful exploration of that gorgeous body.

All that in five seconds flat.

It took another five to come to his senses.

Reel it in, he warned himself, curling his fingers into

fists. As much as he wanted Tessa—and, oh, God, he wanted her—he was still struggling to get his head around everything that'd happened over the past few days. Given how things had gone down with Jackrabbit, he knew his judgment was iffy, his reactions edgy.

He was walking a precarious line right now.

If he fell on one side, he'd quite likely grab her up, haul her off and plunge into the glorious depths of a body he'd spent the past few months dreaming about. It'd go too fast for finesse, too wild for appreciation. Hell, the way he was feeling, he wasn't even sure he'd wait for permission.

A plummet down the other side involved emotional declarations, promises and, God help him, possibly even begging.

Neither option was pretty.

A day, he promised himself.

All he needed was another day.

He'd have it all figured out by then. What to do about the charges, how to make up for the damage, where he stood in the fallout. And, of course, which of the emotions flying through his system were real, which were lust mirages and which were spawned from a desperate need to believe that breaking one of his own rules wasn't going to completely jack up his entire life.

By tomorrow night, he'd have a handle on his thoughts, know whether he was acting wisely or reacting emotionally. The former being the goal, the latter would be disastrous.

Sure he had everything settled in his head, he watched Tessa approach, dimly aware of the pretty blonde by her side. The hypnotic sway of Tessa's hips had the skirt fluttering around million-dollar legs, making Gabriel wonder how tight she could wrap those babies around his body. Could she link her feet behind his back to get a good grip?

Of course, she was so tiny, she probably didn't weigh as much as his backpack. Even if he had to slide his hands under that sweet ass of hers to support her while he drove into her body, he didn't figure holding her would slow him down any.

Control.

Gabriel shoved his clenched fists into the pockets of his cargo pants. Both to keep from reaching out for her, and to disguise his growing erection. He tried to channel his lust into his fists to squeeze it away, but they were a little too close to said erection to make moving his fingers very smart.

"Gabriel, hey."

He nodded at Livi's friendly greeting, the trickle of guilt making its way down his spine for being the one here with her instead of Irish, who was stuck cleaning up the mess Gabriel's report had created.

"I thought you were going sailing," Livi continued, reaching him before Tessa did and giving him a quick hug. "At least that's what I heard the burlesque trio say this morning as they hurried out in bikinis."

"I changed my mind and went for a hike instead," he said, not admitting that he'd made that decision when he'd saw them approaching the boat.

His gaze cut to the reason for his disinterest.

Tessa had stopped just a few steps behind Livi. Too far away to touch, but close enough for her scent to wrap around him like a husky whisper on a dark night. Her heavily lashed blue eyes were locked on him, an amused look on her face as if she found it funny that he'd run from a chance to have sex with three women who made their living straddling a long, hard pole.

An offer he wouldn't have been able to refuse if she'd

made it, he admitted to himself. As long as she made it tomorrow, after he'd cleared his head.

"Well, well, if it isn't Romeo," she said in greeting in her usual sexy purr. Her voice, the memory of how she'd used it like a sex toy when they'd talked on the phone, sent a shaft of desire racing through his system.

It wasn't as though he was some sex-crazed teenager, or a horndog sailor hitting shore for the first time in eight months, or a jerk with no sense of tact or style. He could easily control himself.

Tessa slid her tongue over her bottom lip, her eyes doing a slow, thorough inventory of his body with enough heat that he was surprised his clothes didn't burn away.

Okay, so control wouldn't be so easy. But he was a SEAL. He could handle it.

As long as he didn't touch her.

"Hello, angel," he said, offering a warm smile from a safe distance. "Gorgeous as always, I see. Red suits you."

Of course, he was pretty sure she could make burlap look sexy.

"Well, it's no bikini," she demurred with a sweep of those lashes before offering a wicked smile. "Or, you know, a towel."

Gabriel rocked back on his heels, his smile growing almost as wide as his dick was hard at the reminder of their phone call and her offer to remove his towel with her teeth.

"I was getting ready to show Tessa around the hotel," Livi said, sounding amused. Maybe. He couldn't tear his eyes off Tessa's face to check. "You know, for all that wedding stuff we've got going on."

"Right. Wedding stuff," he repeated absently as his eyes wandered over Tessa's face. She looked the same, he realized with a slight frown. He wasn't sure why that surprised him. Maybe because it felt as if so much had changed between them that there'd be a sign of some sort.

"Mmm, wedding stuff. And maybe some lingerie shopping. I saw the cutest little boutique on our way here," Tessa said, the wicked edge on her smile making him nervous.

Him.

Nervous.

Holy crap.

Gabriel ran his hand over his buzzed hair, wondering what the hell was going on. Maybe the California air was finally getting to him.

"Oh, Olivia, there you are," someone called out.

Both women winced, a move Gabriel mentally echoed as he recognized the voice. He'd spent more than his share of time with Pauline in the past day and a half.

"Uh-oh," Tessa murmured. "I haven't had enough to drink to deal with your mother yet. I'm going to steal Romeo, 'kay? We'll do the wedding stuff later this afternoon."

"Sure," Livi said, her face tightening at her mother's approach. "Half the things will probably have changed by then anyway."

"You want me to stick around?" Tessa offered quietly. "Divide and deflect?"

"No, no." Her smile easy again, Livi shooed them away. "Go, hurry. Otherwise she'll have you counting place settings or chasing down the right shade of cornflower ribbons."

What the hell was cornflower? Before he could ask, Tessa tilted her head toward the balcony.

"You don't want to know," she murmured, crooking her finger to indicate that he should come along.

He followed her out of the lobby, grinning when her

steps quickened as Pauline's strident voice asked where they were going. The increased speed did amazing things for her hips, the red fabric of her skirt swaying temptingly, right there in touching distance. His palms itched to cup those hips, to pull her tight against his body and see how that butt fit against his erection. His eyes slid down her shapely legs to the spiked heels, noting they were at least four inches high and would bring her butt in perfect alignment with the hardness of his eager dick.

Before they reached the balcony, she angled right. He followed her up the short flight of stairs, wondering where they were going but enjoying the view too much to ask.

After the second short flight of stairs, she paused in a long, semidarkened hallway that appeared deserted and turned.

Her eyes glinted with a light that Gabriel recognized.

He did a quick recon, noting that there were only three doors in the hallway, that the silence indicated they were completely alone and that his chances for lasting until tomorrow were somewhere this side of slim and none.

Still, he had to try.

"Maybe we shouldn't have left Livi," he said. "I kinda feel as though I should help as much as I can since Mitch pulled extra duty."

Especially since he was directly responsible for that extra duty.

"Livi's fine," Tessa assured him, her voice low as she gave him a long, slow look from head to toe. "If we're there, she'll feel as if she has to be polite and put on a show that her mother isn't a bully who took lessons from Attila the Hun."

Tessa reached out to skim her fingers over his cheek, her smile calculating. But not in the way he'd seen on other women. She didn't look as if she were trying to figure out what she could get out of him, what he was worth or how well he'd look for show-and-tell. Tessa looked as though she was trying to figure out just exactly what she'd like to do first to drive him crazy on the way to fulfilling his every sexual fantasy.

Gabriel barely resisted the urge to check his brow to see if he was sweating.

"You know her pretty well." He stopped to clear his throat, then tried again. "Why don't we get a drink and you can fill me in on everything I need to know to navigate the treacherous wedding waters this week."

"Why don't we talk about that later," Tessa said, her fingers trailing down his chest now, swirling in teasing little circles. "I think we have a few other things to discuss now."

Discuss.

Discussion was good.

Some of the tension drained from Gabriel's shoulders. Sure, it pooled in his dick, but he figured that'd recede eventually. Maybe.

"What did you want to discuss?" he asked, ready for anything that'd distract from his hard-on.

"This," she said, holding up one finger so an old-fashioned iron skeleton key dangled.

"What's this for?"

"My room."

About damned time, his body shouted. *Oh, hell no*, his mind yelled right back. But his erection was giving a happy salute behind his zipper, easily drowning them both out.

Gabriel glanced at the door just a reach away. Then he looked at the woman standing in front of him with a look on her face that promised to introduce him to a myriad of decadently sensual pleasures on the other side of that door.

He'd never been more tempted in his life.

Still, he'd made a decision. And given the results of

giving way on his last decision, he knew he'd better stick with his resolve.

He'd just have to do so with enough charisma and appeal that she didn't mind waiting. Not an easy task if she was as hot for him as he was for her. But hey, he had an abundance of charm. He'd make it work.

His smile shifted from edgy to easy, his body language set at about the same heat level as a friendly hug.

"Tessa—"

Before he could finish his sentence, or even figure out what he was going to say, her mouth was on his. Her lips were so full, so soft.

Her taste filled his senses, addictively rich with just a hint of sweetness.

Her scent wrapped around him like darkness on a moonless night. Alluring and dangerous.

Just one kiss, he decided.

Lips on lips, nothing more.

Then her tongue swept over his mouth.

Like a flame to a fuse, he went off.

A blast of need more powerful that a C-4 explosion flashed, destroying his resolve, flattening his resistance. Screw his rules. To hell with mistakes. He didn't give a damn anymore.

All he cared about was Tessa.

He thrust his tongue into her mouth, taking control and setting the pace. Fast, hard, intense. Just the way he liked it.

Tessa met his passion with her own, her hands seeming to be everywhere at once. Cupping his biceps, gripping his shoulders, scraping over his pecs and grabbing his ass.

It wasn't until he had her backed up against the wall that he realized that he'd filled his own hands with her lush breasts. And more impressive, that she'd hiked herself up high enough to wrap those silken legs of hers around his waist.

The move brought her core flush against his throbbing dick, his pants and her bunched-up skirt the only things keeping him from heaven.

Heaven with his very own angel.

Groaning, Gabriel shifted to slide his mouth over her cheek, nipping at the delicate curve of her ear before scraping his teeth down her throat.

"Somebody could come at anytime," he murmured, burying his face in the curve of her neck and breathing in her seductive scent.

Her foot slid higher, her stiletto rasping along the back of his thigh with enough pressure that he could feel the sharp edge through his jeans.

His dick echoed his groan with an aching throb.

"I'm betting that somebody is me," she purred, her head falling back against the wall to give him better access to her throat and, he was pleased to note, the glory that was her chest. Full and ample, her breasts pressed tightly against her dress, the red fabric cutting into her lush flesh. "And that time could be any moment now if you put those clever hands of yours to work."

As if he was in a trance—or simply knocked stupid from the explosion of lust between them—Gabriel watched as his finger traced along the edge of her dress. For a second he marveled at the contrast of his skin against the porcelain white of hers, the hardness of his hand against the softness of her breast.

Desperate to see more, he slipped his knuckle under the fabric, pulling it down until the sweet pink of her aureole was visible. Damn. He had to lean closer, had to taste her.

As soon as his tongue touched that pale delicacy he had to have more. Forgetting that they were in a public hallway, he hooked his finger between her breasts and tugged harder, nearly ripping her dress in half. Black lace wrapped over those breasts, highlighting rather than hiding their beauty.

Damn. Passion surged, need spiking through him so fast that he had to close his eyes for a moment to get control.

"Oh, yeah," she gasped, her legs tightening around his waist. "Those are some very clever hands."

His clever hands slid under her skirt, reveling in the taut smoothness of her silken thigh before squeezing her butt. He ran kisses over her breasts while his hand meandered around from her butt to dip between her thighs.

It was like discovering heaven. A wet, hot heaven.

Gabriel wasn't sure how he managed it, but somehow he got the key into the door, twisted it and shoved the carved wood open. It ricocheted off the wall, almost hitting him in the shoulder as he angled Tessa inside. He was pretty sure he closed it. At least, he heard a loud bang. But he couldn't spare it enough attention to check.

Instead, he gave himself over to Tessa.

Every delicious inch of her and the mind-blowing sensations she was eliciting in his body.

Her fingers combed over his chest, scraping gently before curling over his shoulders to grip him tight as she angled herself higher. Her heels dug into the small of his back, her body curved into his in a way that made him curse the layers of clothes separating him from her wet heat.

It took two tugs to send what was left of her dress and bra flying across the room, leaving that warm, silken flesh bare for his mouth. Cupping one full breast in his hand, he leaned closer, running his tongue around her aureole in ever-tightening circles until he reached the delicious center. He sucked her nipple, pebbled taut, between his lips, flicking it with his tongue.

"More," she demanded, her breath coming faster in time with her hands as they raced over his shoulders, tugging at his shirt hard enough to send the buttons flying.

"Take it," he said, his words husky against her other breast. He shifted so she was balanced between his body and the wall, leaving his hands free to cup both her breasts. His mouth moved from one to the other, hot and wet.

"Oh, yeah," she moaned as her hands found bare flesh, her nails scraping like delicate fire down his abs. Then she grabbed hold of his chest with one hand, angling her body away so there was enough space between them for her hand to slip down and free his zipper.

Already on fire, Gabriel's body hit inferno as her nails skimmed his rock-hard dick.

He yanked her dress out of his way, the sound of ripping fabric echoing over their labored breath. Their arms tangled and bodies twisted as he shoved his shirt and pants out of the way and sent Tessa's panties flying. Somehow he managed to sheath himself with a condom before Tessa's legs tightened again, her heels pressing against the small of his back.

"Mmm, you're definitely worth the wait," Tessa said with a little growl. "But I'm through waiting. So you need to do me, lover. And do me now."

Oh, yeah. Need pounded through him, but one of her words echoed over pleasure's demand.

Lover.

"Say my name," he demanded.

"Do me first," she teased, her words muffled because her mouth was skimming over his shoulder. She punctuated the demand with a bite sharp enough to send a shaft of desire through him so strong he thrust forward.

He barely caught himself.

"Say it," he growled, his tense body poised for entry.

"Romeo," she breathed, slowly lifting those heavy lids and giving him a challenging look.

"Say it," he repeated, his fingers sliding between her thighs to gently flick her swollen bud. When she didn't respond, he gave it a little pinch.

"Gabriel," she gasped. Her nails dug into his shoulders; her back arched.

"Gabriel."

It only took a single thrust to send him to heaven.

Oh, God.

   Oh, God.

   Oh, God.

The chant rang through Tessa's mind. Pleasure surged through her body with more power than anything she'd ever felt. The trembling started in her core and spread, rippling through her system in ever-widening waves of delight.

He was incredible.

Her hands gripped Gabriel's shoulders, fingers kneading with every plunge of his body. He was so big, so hard, every thrust slid against her G-spot, filling her with pleasure so powerful she was shaking.

Her back was anchored to the wall, so she used the pressure of her heels to pull herself tighter against his body with each thrust until they were slamming together.

His fingers pinched her nipples, his mouth taking hers in a sloppy, wet kiss that was all tongue and heat.

And that was all it took to send her over the edge. Her body exploded. Pleasure spun out of control, spiraling through her so fast she was dizzy. Gasping for breath, her head fell back against the wall, her orgasm going on and on and on.

Gabriel thrust faster, plunging in and out.

Harder.

More.

So incredibly good that he sent Tessa over another time.

"Gabriel," she gasped.

He growled. She felt his muscles tighten, his thrust hitch.

"Gabriel," she breathed again.

His moan reverberated through her, his body freezing before plunging again.

Having this kind of power over him sent Tessa spiraling up again. Need tightened in her core.

"Gabriel," she gasped, grinding against him.

Then he thrust again. So hard, so deep, she swore she felt him all the way to her heart as he exploded.

"Gabriel, Gabriel, Gabriel," she panted as she came again with an intensity that blew her mind.

The room went black against her closed eyelids, her body so numb with pleasure she wasn't sure if she'd passed out or not. It might have been five minutes, it might have been five hours before Tessa could feel her body again. She pried her eyes open, too overwhelmed to even be surprised that they were on the bed, Gabriel's body warm over hers.

She'd known he was talented.

A man didn't earn a reputation like his without pleasing an incredibly high number of women. She'd spent the past month with his own words about pleasure zones ringing through her mind, keeping her awake at night wondering which zones would give her the most pleasure if he played with them.

But she'd had no idea just how talented he was.

"Angel?"

"Hmm?" she murmured, struggling to hear him through the roaring in her ears.

"We're not finished," he growled against her throat, his teeth scraping a gentle trail across her shoulder.

"We're not?" Tessa couldn't even raise her head, let alone imagine going another round.

Then his mouth found her breast, his teeth working her still-throbbing, deliciously swollen nipple.

"Not even close. I've wanted you for what feels like a lifetime. It's going to take a lifetime to get my fill."

With that he slid lower, his mouth an erotic magnet for pleasure as it moved over her belly. His fingers teased and tweaked her nipples, flicking then rubbing in time with the kisses he spread lower and lower.

Tessa gasped as his jaw pressed her thighs apart, his breath warm on her still-wet, oversensitized nether lips.

She wasn't sure how she'd gotten naked—she barely remembered how they'd gotten into the hotel room.

All she knew was that she had never felt this way. Never before, in all her experiences, had she ever been so far gone with passion that she lost the ability to think, to reason.

All she could do was feel.

And, oh, God, she felt good.

As if he'd heard her thoughts and took them as a challenge, Gabriel's tongue swept over her clitoris, sipping gently before sliding into her trembling core. His fingers worked magic while his tongue danced so seductively that it took Tessa a few moments to realize the mewling sounds she heard were her.

"Come for me, baby," he whispered against her thigh. "I want to taste you while you go over."

Ooh, God.

Tessa's orgasm came in waves, each one bigger, more

powerful than the last. Pleasure pounded over her, sweeping her away to a place she'd never been.

Overwhelmed, she pressed her eyes tight to try to keep the sudden tears from falling.

Gabriel gently kissed his way up her body, worshipping her back to earth with a sweetness that blew her mind.

Her head was spinning, her body melting into a sea of sexual delight. She'd never felt this way. So sated with pleasure that she knew nothing would ever feel this good again. How had he done that? Tessa surreptitiously rubbed her finger under her eyes to wipe away the teary mascara smudges even as he poised over her with a look of awe on his face that told her he was as hooked as she was.

Pretending that didn't terrify her, Tessa lifted her body, her hips thrusting high and hard to welcome him in.

Perfect, was all she could think.

He was so awesomely perfect.

TESSA WOKE LATER, her body draped over Gabriel's, her bones a melted puddle and her mind pure mush. It took her a few seconds of blinking to realize that dark had fallen and she wasn't still asleep.

She still didn't move, though. She couldn't. How many times had they made love? Three? Five? She'd lost track.

Something did seep through the pleasure-drugged fog, though.

She'd been right.

He was good.

So good that he took sex past the realm of pleasure into the land of mind-blowing oh-my-God awesomeness.

That was the kind of sex she could get hooked on.

She didn't know if it was his mouth and the wicked things he could do with his tongue or his hands.

Oh, his hands. Her thighs trembled, the swollen folds of her center throbbing at the memory of those hands.

The man had some amazing hands. Almost as amazing as his body. She took a deep breath, her lungs the only thing she could move, and reveled in the sensations of that body beneath hers.

Oh, yeah. He was good.

Good enough to be dangerous.

Her muscles, molten just seconds ago, stiffened as fear trickled through her system.

That kind of dangerous was scary.

Then Gabriel—no, not Gabriel. If she were going to keep from freaking out, he needed to stay Romeo.

Then *Romeo's* hand curved over her butt, giving it a gentle squeeze. And all the fears faded, the worries, the crazy thoughts about getting up and running away didn't stand a chance against the pleasure of his touch.

"More," she urged, forcing herself to lift her head. It wasn't until she did that she realized it had been resting on his incredibly toned, deliciously sculpted abs.

A wicked smile curving her lips, she found her second wind. And used it to kiss her way over those abs and up to take him into her mouth.

As distractions went, it was delicious.

11

GABRIEL HAD HAD a lot of sex in his life.

He considered himself something of an expert at it, actually. Because of that expertise, he could easily discern the difference between good-enough sex—the kind that relaxed the body and cleared the mind—and great sex, the kind that blew the mind and pushed the boundaries of pleasure.

But sex with Tessa?

His gaze cut across the moonlit beach, easily finding her in the crowd dancing around the bonfire. Her hair was up tonight, swirled into some sort of tangle of curls that made her look as if she'd just rolled out of bed.

Sex with Tessa was beyond anything he'd experienced before.

He'd expected it to be intense. She was a woman who nurtured her sexuality; she was an expert in the games between the sexes. He'd seen for himself how responsive and sensual she was during the myriad of sexy-talk sessions they'd shared.

He'd been ready for great.

He'd been prepared for mind-blowing.

He'd even anticipated a little addiction and need.

Yeah. He'd been ready for all of that.

But the sweetness? The protective feeling he'd had while watching her sleep? And that possessive urge to grab her tight so she could never get away?

Those had been a shock.

He was a man who specialized in explosions.

But what'd happened between them yesterday—every one of the seven times—had leveled him in every way.

But Tessa?

His scowl deepened.

He'd never slithered out of a woman's bed without a word. He considered that disrespectful. And he'd certainly never had a woman leave his—usually they had to be pried out with the equivalent of an emotional crowbar.

So he didn't figure he could write off his morning-after experience to karma or paybacks. And while he readily acknowledged that Tessa had her own sexual MO, he didn't think she made a habit of sneaking out of a man's bed without a word, either.

But she had his.

He did know that waking that morning ready for another round of mind-blowing sex only to find himself alone had totally sucked. It'd sucked even harder to spend the day missing Tessa at every turn. He walked into the hotel lounge to be told she'd left a few minutes before to lead the wedding guests on a hike over the island. He'd joined the hike and found out she'd asked one of Livi's trainers to lead the hike so she could join the bride at the spa. He'd looked for her at lunch but apparently there had been a flower-petal emergency. Everywhere she was supposed to be, she suddenly wasn't.

It didn't take intelligence training to know she was avoiding him.

He clenched his teeth as frustration and anger stirred up a tasteless cocktail in his belly.

He'd known she'd do this.

Dammit, he'd called it two months ago. That was why he'd launched Operation Romance. Because he'd been damned if he'd be tossed into her easily dismissed pile of discarded lovers. Because he'd known there was more to the spark between them than just hot sex.

Images of the previous day and night flashed through his mind—hot bodies sliding together in a perfect symphony of tangled limbs, escalating passion and out-of-control orgasms—and forced him to amend that to incredibly hot sex.

This thing between them was about more than sex, though.

Operation Romance had done more than delay sexual gratification. It'd proved that he and Tessa truly connected. They fit. From their tastes in entertainment to their personalities, their devotion to fitness to their love of sushi. He felt inspired when he talked to her. As if there was more to his life than his career. He felt at peace when he was with her, as if he'd finally found that something that'd been missing for so long that he hadn't even realized it was gone.

Apparently what Operation Romance hadn't done, though, was achieve its long-term objective. To keep Tessa hooked after the ecstatic cries of her orgasms had faded.

Her sneaking out this morning had convinced him that despite everything they had between them—all of the potential for more—she'd still walk away.

She'd throw away what they had without a backward glance.

What in the hell was her issue?

Gabriel would happily change his Navy rating to join the IDC if it meant he could find out why. Leaving explosives for Information Dominance Corps would be a small price to pay to know what had gone wrong.

Gabriel's gaze easily found Tessa again. Shoulder to shoulder with a couple others on a log, she looked as if she was having fun. But even from a distance he could see the wall she put up between herself and everyone else.

He knew firsthand just how effective that wall was. Hell, he'd constructed a carefully planned operation to get past it, hadn't he? ·

Yet another plan he hadn't followed through on.

His fists clenching and unclenching, Gabriel tried to shake off the sick feeling in his gut, to squeeze it away.

He'd give a lot to blow something up right now.

TESSA HAD BLOWN IT.

She'd thought she was so smart.

Seduce Romeo, use the distraction of sex between them as a buffer to get through this week. Keep it light and easy and, yes, maybe prove that she was still the same ol' Tessa. A naughty man-eater who could seduce a guy stupid and walk away without another thought.

She'd managed the seducing him part incredibly well.

The memory of their lovemaking sent shivers of desire through her body so strong they actually drowned out the fear.

Because the seduction had gone too well. Sex with Gabriel had been the most powerful thing she'd ever felt. The most incredible time she'd ever had.

She'd been worried she'd lose herself in him.

Instead, she'd found herself.

Curled up in a quiet corner of the hotel veranda, she watched the lunch crowd disperse, grateful that there was no sign of Gabriel. She'd been avoiding him since she'd woke in his arms yesterday, the two of them wrapped together as though they'd found heaven. She'd lain there imagining the two of them wrapped together for the rest of their lives, each of them completing the other.

And then she'd totally freaked out.

Thinking that a little distance between them until she

could handle the unfamiliar emotions ricocheting through her system would be best, she'd sneaked out.

Her gaze shifted to her shoes, a cheer-me-up gift she'd bought herself yesterday while working on that distance. She had four more pairs up in her room. But no amount of shoes, shopping or partying had changed her feelings about Gabriel.

Unable to sit any longer, she got to her feet and paced by the railing, the ocean beyond doing nothing to ease her turmoil. It was a good thing that her specialty was on writing about the chase and not the relationship. Fitting, since she had no idea how to have one.

As if on cue, her cell phone rang a jive beat.

"Maeve," she answered, grateful for the distraction. "Hey."

"Whoa, I didn't figure you'd pick up," Maeve said, her surprise coming through the line loud and clear. "I thought you'd be all tied up in wedding stuff."

"Nope, I'm totally free," she said, thinking back to her visit to the florist that morning with Livi and Mitch's mom, Denise. It'd been her first experience as an invisible person. "Why did you call if you didn't think I'd answer?"

She was pretty sure she knew, though.

In case she was right, Tessa moved away from the cheerful brunch crowd, crossing the balcony toward the stairs.

"I was going to leave you a message. Not that messages are a good way to impart this sort of thing, but I figured voice mail was better than email. And texts? Those always suck. Might as well develop a texting font called screw-you-I'm-too-busy-to-care."

Her breath tight in her chest, Tessa dropped to sit on the top step, the ocean a blur in the distance.

"Maeve," she said quietly, forcing the words past the knot in her throat. "You're babbling."

"Right." The redhead's shaky breath whooshed over the phone line, making Tessa shiver. "Another takeover offer came in this morning."

"I thought we had a plan. Revamp our format, up our game and hold out for more money."

Scowling at the ocean, Tessa wondered why people couldn't slow the hell down. She was in the middle of this ridiculous identity crisis. How was she supposed to figure herself out if everything kept changing?

"I guess word got out. Two other media groups contacted Jared yesterday, so he figured he'd up the game a little and gave all three companies our tentative proposal. The big boys were seriously impressed with the new direction and changes. Either that or they just got freaky over competition. Whatever it was, they came in immediately with a new offer."

Typical. Tessa rolled her eyes.

Then Maeve laid out the offer.

Holy crap. There was nothing typical about that kind of money.

Tessa's brain shut down.

She couldn't think.

She could barely breathe.

Her head buzzed in time with the tiny dots dancing in front of her eyes.

"Tess?"

"You're serious?" Tessa said, repeating the dollar amount. Her share was at least ten times more than she made in a year. "That's a real offer?"

"Real enough that Jared wanted to bring you home to nail down the contracts before they change their minds. I told him next week was soon enough, though."

Tessa couldn't blame him. The deal sounded too good to be true. But even her usual cynicism couldn't stand up to the hope unfurling in her belly. This offer was big enough to not only give her breathing room to figure out what to do with her life, but it was also impressive enough that nobody hearing it would think she was a talentless fraud. Which was even more important than the money, she realized.

"How's Jared handling it?" she asked.

"Last time I saw him, he was breathing into a paper bag."

Tessa didn't have a paper bag, so she dropped her head between her knees and tried to breathe.

"We have to accept the offer." Maeve's voice was faint but echoed through Tessa's head, as if she was talking from a cave. Not surprising given the angle of the phone. "You agree? We have to take it?"

Her head spinning a little slower now, Tessa slowly straightened to stare at the wild dance of the waves over the ocean's surface.

"Well, we don't have to do anything," she said, grateful to hear a little confidence in her voice.

"But?"

"But we'd be crazy not to."

"Okay, that's not all, then," Maeve said after giving a relieved sigh so big, Tessa was surprised it didn't fluff her hair.

"There's more?" Unable to sit any longer, Tessa slid out of her shoes. She wasn't about to mess up the darling canvas platforms by wearing them on the beach. Scooping them up, she hurried down the stairs toward the beach.

"There's more. Are you sitting down?"

"Sitting? You're kidding, right? I feel like dancing." Tessa kicked up a little sand with a laugh, feeling as if some of her fears scattered along with the tiny grains.

Then Maeve told her what *more* was.

Tessa didn't even feel her darling canvas platforms slide

from her fingers. Her knees gave out, her butt hitting the sand with a thud.

She didn't know if she responded. She didn't remember hanging up. All she could do was stare at the water and wait for the buzzing in her head to abate.

Eventually she shivered, realizing the sun was setting and she'd been plopped here for who knew how long. Before she could get up, a shadow fell.

Out of the corner of her eye she noted two very large feet encased in a pair of military-style hiking boots. She didn't recognize the footwear, but the heat pooling in her belly recognized the wearer.

Still, she'd suffered a shock. Maybe her belly was wrong. Tessa shielded her eyes with one hand, letting her gaze climb a pair of deliciously long legs clad in worn denim, then rest for a moment on the zipper—behind which lay the key to heaven—before she resumed her inspection with abs worth drooling over, a glorious chest covered in black cotton and shoulders draped in a loose jacket. Her gaze finally reached the face etched forever in her brain. And, if she wasn't careful, on her heart.

A face that was sporting a scowl.

Tessa frowned. Had she ever seen him scowl before?

"Your alert must be faulty," Romeo said, the chilly distance in his voice sending a trickle of guilt down her back. Like the scowl, that was new.

And apparently new wasn't always a good thing.

Tessa frowned, dropping her hand to stare at the ocean again. Was new ever a good thing? She'd always thought so, but lately new seemed to be tossing her life into a crazy whirlwind, mixing everything up and leaving her confused.

A part of her wanted to jump up and grab Romeo, to

share her news while leading him in a frenzied happy dance over the sand.

A part of her just wanted to grab him.

The little voice in her head warned her to keep quiet, to decide what she wanted and how she felt before sharing her news. Maybe even verify a few things. Otherwise she might end up looking like an idiot.

Instead of just feeling like one.

She slid a sideways glance at Romeo's feet and sighed.

Yeah. She'd definitely screwed up. She just wasn't sure if the screwup had been in leaving him in bed yesterday. Or in joining him there in the first place.

"Are you okay?" he asked, the chill replaced with concern.

Was she? Tessa blinked, her brow creasing as she tried to decide.

"What alert?" she finally asked after replaying his greeting a couple times in her head.

"The one that warns you that I'm approaching. You know, so you can be somewhere else."

Busted.

Any other time, Tessa would have laughed.

All she could manage right now was a wave of her hand, though.

"So what's wrong? You upset that I finally caught up with you?"

More like upset that all she wanted to do right now was curl into his arms for a hug. And not even a prelude-to-sex hug. A real, filled-with-affection-and-support hug.

"You might find this difficult to believe, but not everything revolves around you," Tessa said defensively. Except that some things did revolve around him, which meant that while she might not be willing to offer an explanation, she did owe him an apology. Sighing, Tessa offered a remorseful shrug. "It's really nothing. I'm fine. I just have some things to think through."

Hoping he'd get the hint, she turned to stare at the ocean again. But the view didn't soothe. Instead, the wild waves crashing over rocks added to the urgent sense of turmoil pounding through her system. What was she supposed to do?

Apparently she wasn't going to figure it out sitting here. So she got to her feet and rubbed her hands over her arms to chase away the sudden goose bumps, before bending down to scoop her shoes out of the sand.

"Did you want to walk on the beach?" he offered quietly. "It might help you clear your head."

"Are you going to chew me out for not sticking around yesterday?" she asked, knowing she deserved it but not able to deal with that just yet.

"How about I hold off on the lecture and just offer to be a strong shoulder, a sounding board or maybe even a friend of sorts," he said. His dark gaze was mellow, his tone quiet. Tessa wondered if this was his attempt at innocuous. She'd tell him it was useless, since a man with his level of sex appeal, power and energy could never be considered harmless. But he was so sweet, all she could do was smile.

"Sure. A walk on the beach would be nice." Following his gesture, she made her way toward the water. Too chilly to sunbathe, the beach was sparsely populated, making for an easy trek to the ocean's edge.

Enjoying the feel of wet sand beneath her bare feet, she focused on the wind in her hair and the sound of the ocean, letting them soothe her in a way she'd never realized nature could.

She slid a surreptitious glance at the man walking quietly alongside her.

Well, nature, or Gabriel.

The longer they walked, the more stress fell away. It wasn't until they'd reached a place in front of one of the upscale resorts that she realized that the odd feeling in her belly was peace. Just the thought of it almost made her trip in the sand.

"Break?" Gabriel suggested.

"Sure." Glancing at the plush lounge chairs set back from the water's edge, then down at the satin fabric of her long maxi dress with its brilliant turquoise and fuchsia flowers, she shrugged and dropped gracefully to the sand.

A position her butt was getting familiar with today.

"Here's fine," she said, smiling up at him. She gave a rueful nod to the hut-style building just beyond the lounge chairs with its little windows boarded up. "Too bad the bar is closed."

She could definitely use a drink.

"That's okay," he said, dropping down next to her, settling his long legs straight out beside her. Then he pulled a small bottle out of his jacket pocket. "I brought wine."

Tessa laughed in delight.

"Aren't you handy," she said. "But I don't have a glass."

"Live dangerously," he suggested with a wicked grin. "Chug it from the bottle."

So she did, appreciating the gesture and the excellent vintage. When she offered him a drink, he shook his head to indicate that this one was all hers.

He was so damned good-looking, leaning back with his elbows in the sand, his feet crossed casually at the ankles as he stared out at the water. His entire demeanor was mellow.

She frowned, looking closer as she realized that there was a whole lot of stress going on under that mellow. She'd been so self-involved that she hadn't seen it before.

She wasn't so self-involved that she thought those frown lines were because of her, though.

"Are you okay?" she asked quietly, reaching out for just a moment to skim her fingers over the back of his hand.

"I'm watching Mother Nature's glory with a beautiful woman by my side. How could I not be okay?"

Tessa's lips twitched.

Charm.

The guy must bathe in it.

She wanted to push the issue. To insist he open up, share his worries so she could try to help. Either that or pull him close into a soothing hug.

"I'll bet you were a great Boy Scout," she heard herself saying instead.

Better, since asking emotional questions would obligate her to answer them in return. And she wasn't quite that peaceful yet.

"Me?" He laughed. "The closest I've come to being a Scout is the SEAL team."

Tessa frowned when his smile faded. A trickle of worry seeped down her spine. His job, his entire world—it was so dangerous. Was there something wrong with his SEAL team? She opened her mouth, wanting to ask, needing to be reassured that his safety wasn't in danger.

But she couldn't ask.

"I'm surprised you weren't a Boy Scout," she said, opting for the chicken route once again. "You've got that always-prepared thing down pat."

"Scouting wasn't big on the reservation. Later I was living on the streets more often than not so would have missed the meetings." He shrugged.

"Reservation?" Fascinated, Tessa shifted in the sand so she could more clearly see his face.

"I spent my first handful of years in and out of foster

care until my grandfather found me. He took me to live with him on the reservation," he said, his eyes distant as he watched the stars overhead. "He died when I was eleven."

"I'm so sorry." Unused to offering sympathy but unable not to, Tessa reached out again to lay her hand over the back of his. She gave it a quick squeeze, but before she could pull away, he turned his over so their fingers entwined.

Telling herself it was to offer comfort and not because his touch sent delicious zings of sexual delight through her body, Tessa left her hand there.

"He'd lived a full life," Gabriel said with another shrug. "And he taught me a lot. I learned the importance of setting rules I could live with. He was big on dedicating oneself to a path and living it with honor."

His voice took on that edge again, frustration and pain layered with anger.

"Are you okay?" she asked, her fingers tightening on his.

"Fine."

"You don't sound fine."

He gave her an arch look.

"Why don't we discuss what's bothering you first?" he suggested. "You know, pretend we have a real relationship where we share these little things."

"Sarcasm," she observed, totally in sync with the deflective benefits of well-placed snark. "Nicely done."

He grinned, tilting his head in thanks. And, she realized, as a dare for her to step up and accept that they were really in that relationship he'd mentioned.

Relationship. Her feet twitched, her mind screaming at her to grab her shoes and run. But she'd run yesterday. She'd like to claim that doing the same thing twice made her predictable, and what woman wanted that label? But the reality was, she'd been miserable after running. And worse, she realized with a pang, she'd hurt Gabriel.

Did that mean he was right? They were in a relationship?

Okay, fine.

She took a deep breath, hoping it'd smother the panic clawing its way through her nervous system.

"I'm sorry I blew you off. Earlier and yesterday. I was…" The words stuck in her throat, forcing her to clear it before she could continue. "Us, together, it was amazing."

"And amazing makes you run?"

There was no judgment in his voice, no anger on his face. Just acceptance and a sort of understanding that almost made her cry.

"Amazing is a little scary," she admitted quietly.

"Yeah." He squeezed her hand. That gentle pressure said more than a thousand words, letting Tessa know that he understood, that he felt exactly the same.

"We're selling *Flirtatious*," she admitted, surprised at how little it hurt to actually say the words aloud.

"Your magazine?"

"Yeah." She explained the history of it, starting with Jared's weird behavior and ending with the call from Maeve. The entire time, he listened with an intensity that made her a little nervous. She was used to surface interactions. It'd be easy to drown in these depths.

"It sounds like a great deal," he said when she'd finished.

"It is," she agreed. Then, after a brief hesitation, she added, "But there's more."

"Tell me." Gabriel shifted onto his side. The way his long body ranged out next to her would have offered a distraction if not for the intense look on his face.

"The media company offered me a job. They want me

to come on board with them and write for three different publications, including *Flirtatious* after they take it over."

"That sounds excellent, but you don't seem to think so," he observed with an astute look.

Tessa hesitated. How did she explain that she already felt enough like a fraud doing something she was supposedly good at someplace with a built-in safety net like *Flirtatious*? The idea of doing more of it, with a bigger audience, was terrifying.

"It's hard for me to share this kind of thing," she said with a rueful laugh. "Hard for me to open up. Admitting problems isn't good for the image."

"The image you present to the world? Or the image you have of yourself?"

"Both." She laughed, lifting her free hand in the air as if to say there was really no difference.

"Would it help if I tell you that I see a lot more than an image when I look at you?" he asked. "I see a strong woman, a sexy one who knows her own worth and demands that the world respect that. I see a woman with a wicked sense of a humor, deep wells of compassion and a huge heart. One who puts friends first, protects herself at all costs and who can do some very, very interesting things with her tongue."

She laughed at that last part, trying not to squirm over the rest. Whether it was his smile, or the fact that she needed to distract her from the fact that she was blushing— something she couldn't ever remember doing before—she decided to confess.

"I don't know if I'll be good at it. Writing my columns, the articles, they've become more difficult over the past year. I feel as though I'm just recycling the same old thing, relying on stale formulas and internet alerts instead of sharing something worthwhile." She stopped short of saying she felt like a failure, thinking that he was a smart guy, he could figure that part out himself. "But it's a great opportunity, a chance to make a lot more money and reach so many more readers. Fame, fortune… I'd be a fool to say no, wouldn't I?"

"Will they want you to write the exact same type of content as you have been?"

She hadn't asked. But if Jared had shut her down based on reader expectations, she couldn't imagine the new publishers would be any different. Frowning at their joined hands, Tessa shrugged. "It's what I'm known for."

"But is it what you want to remain known for? You're great at what you do, angel. Don't doubt that. You bring a tongue-in-cheek humor to a minefield that a lot of people are struggling to navigate, and you do it in a way that makes them feel good about themselves. But if you feel as though you've tapped it out, maybe it's time to expand the field. Not leave it, but expand it."

Tessa felt little tingles of excitement. She could so totally do that. Branch out a little, maybe delve into other topics. That didn't mean she'd be good at them, though.

The tingles took on a pained edge.

What if she was as much of a fraud writing about throwing parties or finding the perfect pair of boots as she was at flirting?

"What if they don't want that?" she asked with a frown, wanting to drop her head into her hands and scream. Or run for the nearest therapist's couch for an overhaul.

"Sometimes I think we get so hooked on what we're known for, so comfortable in our persona, that we're afraid to make changes. Even when not making changes hurts."

Tessa waited for him to continue. To tell her exactly what she should do. Did she take the offer as is, did she push them to expand her assignments before she took it? Or did she simply walk away?

But he didn't say anything else. He just watched.

And then she understood.

She was lousy at taking advice. If he told her what to do, she'd throw up a million excuses. Either that or go in the opposite direction.

"You understand me a little too well for my own good," Tessa admitted nervously. But there was a warm sort of joy in her heart that kept the nerves from getting out of hand.

"The way you feel about your image I feel about my reputation." He shot her a wicked smile. "Despite our rough start, I have a reputation for being damned good at what I do, being easy to get along with and dependable to work with."

She nodded. She'd seen him with Mitch, with his other team members, often enough to see the respect and trust they all had for each other.

"But I can't imagine you'd ever have to worry about anything you do affecting that," she mused.

"Sometimes we don't have a choice. Other factors always come into play. Sometimes the hardest thing to do is accept that. In the SEALs, we train for months before a mission. We play out multiple scenarios, plan for every possibility. Even when we're sure of what we'll be facing, we still develop alternate options."

"And if those other factors screw it all up?" she queried, thinking about how hard it would be to get another job writing if she took this offer and blew it.

"Then we deal with the fallout. That's life," he said, lifting her hand to brush a kiss over her knuckles. "Reputations, images, plans—they all give way to life."

"Aren't you the philosophical one," she teased.

"Go on enough missions, fight enough battles, and it's hard not to be," he said with a one-shouldered shrug.

But she knew it was more than that. His upbringing, his heritage, even that layer of sweetness in his personality—they all played a part.

Tessa swallowed hard as the realization of what he really was hit her.

Sure, he was a gorgeous man.

Sexy, amazingly sexy. Charming, amusing and tempting, undoubtedly.

She already knew that he was incredibly talented in bed. He probably knew things that she, in all her varied experiences both personal and anecdotal, had never experienced. But he was just as schooled in life. He'd dragged himself out of a humble, challenging childhood to embrace a career that he obviously loved. He was one of the elite, which meant he was not just dedicated, but damned good. And he was so smart with insights that saw right to the heart of an issue, no drama or fluff.

But the bottom line was, he was a warrior.

A man driven to protect, to fight, to serve.

A man who understood her, she realized. Inside and out, he saw her for who she was better than she did herself.

And he made her feel incredible about that.

Feeling as though she was on the edge of a terrifying cliff and about to fall into the scariest emotion in the world—love.

"I don't like seeing you upset like this," he told her, looking more angry for her than he had for himself. "Since my usual MO when I see something I don't like is to either fix it, distract from it by having sex or blow it up, I'm in a quandary." Looking as if he was more than willing to settle on the third option, Romeo lifted her hand to his lips and brushed a gentle kiss against her palm.

Her eyes filling at the sweetness of his gesture, Tessa blew a mental kiss at the idea of keeping her heart locked away. And just like that, she felt herself fall over the edge of that cliff. It wasn't a fall, though. It was a headfirst dive into love.

Her laugh was a little husky, her heart pounding with confusion and excitement.

She wasn't ready to tell him yet, though.

So she went with her favorite option instead.

Sex.

"Actually, you can help me out," she told him in a soft voice.

"Yeah?" His smile glinted in the afternoon sun as he reached out to twirl a strand of her hair between his fingers. "What can I do? You name it."

"Me," she said simply. "Do me."

12

DAMNED IF HE didn't feel incredible.

A nice change from the previous night. But hey, great sex, a fabulous view and a woman who made him feel like some kind of hero did amazing things for a guy's mood.

His elbows on the railing overlooking the beach, Gabriel grinned as he watched Tessa work out on the beach with Livi and a handful of other women. With the sun setting behind them, they made quite a picture. Especially Livi's aunt, who was sporting a neon green Mohawk and wearing high-top sneakers.

But as distracting as the neon was, his eyes were locked on his angel. God, she had a gorgeous body. Subtly muscled, she moved through a series of jump-squat lunges with ease. He'd love to get her in a gym and see what she could press. He'd bet she could put a few guys he knew to shame. It was easy to get distracted by the sexy curves and silky skin and miss the strength.

His smile faded as he thought back to their earlier conversation. He wasn't sure what had surprised him more. That she was sporting so many doubts about her talent, or that she'd told him. He'd hid his shock, but he should have offered more solid feedback, maybe some support. He'd meant to. But then she'd distracted him with sex, sending all thoughts—along with most of his blood supply—south of his zipper.

As the group moved on to push-ups Livi went from person to person, adjusting their stance or offering encouragement. But not Tessa. Nope, his angel had perfect form and dived in without instruction or, apparently, any need of praise. He wasn't sure if that spoke to the solidity of their long-term friendship and was a part of their workout style or if the fitness coach simply overlooked Tessa because she was so self-sufficient.

That was why she needed him. To lean on, to depend on. He saw her strengths, appreciated her talents, but he also recognized her vulnerabilities. He knew how to push her, how to encourage her so she felt good about herself even when she didn't realize she'd been feeling bad.

He figured a woman like Tessa could take care of herself financially. She didn't need a man for security and she could readily find plenty to fill her sexual needs— although not nearly as well as he could. But no other man would ever understand her, would ever value her the way he did. And that was what he brought to their relationship.

That, and a desire to spend the rest of his life showing her just how amazing they could be together.

Damn.

Gabriel tried to swallow, but he had no spit.

Dry-mouthed and slightly ill, he stared down at Tessa as she stretched out on the sand.

Was this love?

He suddenly understood why Tessa had run away the day before. Amazing was scary. Scary as hell.

But he'd never backed down from a challenge before. He wasn't about to start now.

Nope, now it was time to up his game and go for the ultimate challenge.

He'd caught his angel.

Now he just had to keep her.

Before he could begin to figure out how, someone stepped up to the railing next to him.

"Yo."

As soon as Gabriel glanced over, his smile faded.

His senses went on high alert, his body tightening and his mind clearing in preparation for whatever was about to hit him. That he'd be hit was a given. That it'd hurt was probable. That he could deal with it?

He gave a mental shrug.

The way he felt right now, he could deal with anything.

"Irish," he greeted with a jerk of his chin. No point in asking what was going on. He'd be told when it was time. "When did you hit the island?"

"Just now," the other man said, looking at the beach with a frown. He jerked his chin toward his pregnant fiancée, who was now stretching her arms overhead as if greeting the sky. "Is she taking it easy?"

"Yeah. I watched the workout. She's dialed it back to mellow." Gabriel angled his head to get a better view of Irish's face. The setting sun cast an orange glow over his features, but didn't disguise the strain. Gabriel glanced back at the women, then at Irish again.

Damn it all to hell.

"Problem?"

"Mission details."

His tension ratcheted up a few tight notches. Gabriel shoved his hands into his pockets and rocked back on his heels, contemplating what those details might be. Bile curdled in his belly as he wondered if he'd ever find out. Details were issued on a need-to-know basis. If he wasn't on the mission, wasn't on the team, he didn't need to know.

Jaw clenched, his eyes shifted back to where Tessa was stretching. Her moves were sinuous and smooth, so enticing that even his anxiety over his career couldn't stop him from getting hard. That was the thing about Tessa.

She was so comfortable in her sexuality that she seduced without trying.

He'd told her that sometimes life didn't offer choices, just fallout. It looked as if he was about to get his. His gut churned but he cleared his head. Worries and fear were deadly in battle and in life.

"Am I in?" he finally asked, needing to know if he'd completely blown it.

"You're solid," Irish assured him.

Gabriel let out the breath he hadn't realized he was holding. But there was something in Irish's tone, an edge that kept him from relaxing completely.

"And?" he persisted. If he were in, asking wasn't against protocol. But the fact that he had to ask rather than Irish readily volunteering the information warned him that there were problems.

"And so am I. We leave in five days." Without another word, without even looking at Gabriel, Irish walked away. Not toward the women, but back inside the hotel.

Irish was supposed to get married in seven days.

Gabriel closed his eyes with a silent groan.

Son of a bitch.

He should have stuck to his guns, followed his rule. He should have stuck with his plan to deal with Jeglinski. It'd seemed like the right thing to do at the time, but look what breaking his rules got him.

He didn't mind taking his knocks when life changed. He owned his own actions. But someone else paying for what he'd done? That went against everything he believed, everything he was.

A movement on the beach caught his eye as Tessa took a bag of towels and mats from Livi. Even from a distance he could see her chiding her friend for doing too much.

He thought back to all of the stories she'd told him, all of the stress she'd gone through over this wedding.

All to make sure her best friend was happy.

That was what she did.

And him?

He ignored his own rules and let people down.

TESSA FELT LIKE the goddess of great sex had sprinkled her with happy dust. Fresh from her shower, revved from her workout, she'd dressed with one thing in mind. Seducing Gabriel again after dinner.

She felt great as she stepped into the hotel lobby.

She gave a little hum when she saw the crowd of cute Navy guys gathered by the check-in desk. Looked as though wedding week was about to get a whole lot more interesting. Of course, she already had her cute Navy guy, so she was already set.

Wouldn't that be a great article?

How, like most things in life, it all came down to the fact that great sex made everything better.

Her smile widened as she sashayed toward the restaurant.

"Tessa, where the hell have you been?"

Her smile stiffened.

Okay, almost everything.

"Hey, Pauline," she greeted, determined to keep a friendly face on for Livi's sake. "I thought the festivities were through for the day. Did I miss an update?"

It was definitely possible, given that she'd set her phone to ignore all notifications of the other woman's emails, texts or messages. Livi would let her know if she wanted something.

"If you'd check your phone you'd know I've been sending SOS messages for the past hour," Pauline said, her face creased tight.

Tessa tensed. Given the older woman's latest cosmetic "touch-up," it took a lot of worry to move that skin.

"What's the matter?"

Pauline shot a quick look around the lobby, then grabbed Tessa's arm to pull her toward the front entrance. Despite being a good half foot shorter, Tessa managed to hold her own with the other woman's long strides. But as soon as they reached the relative privacy of the side garden, she pulled away.

"What's going on?" Her voice iced with fear, Tessa crossed her arms over her chest. "Is Livi okay?"

"Okay? How could she be okay? After everything I've done, all the effort and energy, arranging and rearranging. And now it's ruined." Punctuating every third word with a toss of her hands in the air, Pauline paced the patio. "I didn't say a word against his career because I didn't want to project my fears, my issues with her father, onto her life. I've bit my tongue, I've bent over backward to make this something special for her, something she'd always happily remember, no matter what happened."

When the older woman's rant degenerated into mutters interspersed with creative streams of cussing, Tessa made herself review the rant twice to be sure she had it right.

Finally she took a deep breath and, risking being mowed over, stepped in front of Pauline.

"Just to clarify," she said in her most calming, reasonable tone. "There's an issue with the wedding because of Mitch's job?"

"Job? A banker has a job. A lawyer has a job. Hell, even the garbage man has a job. That isn't a job. It's a death sentence on all relationships it comes into contact with."

Then Pauline scared the hell out of her by bursting into tears and throwing herself into Tessa's arms.

Oh, shit.

Tessa tried to regulate her breathing so she wouldn't hyperventilate as she patted the other woman's back. But Pauline's panic spiked right through the tears with painfully contagious clarity.

"Is Mitch okay?" Tessa asked, needing a few more facts before she let her anxiety take over. "He's safe?"

She took the wet, sniffling grunt as an affirmative.

"But something about his job is going to ruin the wedding?" she asked, hazarding a guess.

The snuffling grunt was louder this time.

"Can we fix it?" Whatever it was, it had to be fixable.

Pauline didn't grunt this time, just sobbed louder. Realizing she wasn't going to get anything useful out of the woman, Tessa cast a frantic look around. Spotting the side door into the bar, she edged closer, Pauline still clinging like a bad date. Tessa managed to catch a waitress's eye and with one hand indicate a drink before pointing at Pauline. The waitress looked a little horrified, but earned a big tip by grabbing the nearest bottle and a glass and hurrying through the door.

"Thanks," Tessa murmured before telling her to charge it to her room.

"Do you need anything else?" the girl asked sympathetically.

Tessa frowned, then nodded. "Can you page Roz Evans to come out here?"

Livi's aunt and mother got along like oil and water, but there was only so much comfort Tessa could handle, and she needed all of it for her friend.

She managed to get Pauline to sit in one of the pretty little bistro chairs, and stuffed a handful of napkins into her hand before pouring a stiff shot of whatever the waitress had brought into a glass.

Tessa knocked it back, then grimaced.

Cheap rum. Nasty, she thought, before refilling the glass for Pauline.

She'd barely convinced the older woman to take it when Roz sauntered through the door.

"I was inspecting their bar and heard my name. What's up?"

"You are," Tessa said, thrusting the bottle into her hands. "I've got to go help Livi."

Three minutes later, her head swirling from the low-grade booze on an empty stomach, Tessa knocked on Livi's door. She'd have made it in two but she'd stopped at the gift shop for emergency chocolate and tissues.

She stuffed her worries into deep freeze, put on her most supportive expression and knocked.

"Hey," Livi greeted when she opened the door. "I thought you said you had dinner plans."

Her arms half-lifted for a hug, Tessa opened her mouth, peered closer at her friend's face, then closed her lips.

Livi didn't look devastated. She didn't even seem upset.

Tessa's arms fell and her shoulders slumped.

What was going on?

"I heard there was a problem," she said slowly, looking around the room in case there was a clue. Or maybe a dead body to hide. She knew if she'd been as Zen as Livi had for this long, she'd definitely have to kill someone.

"A problem? Maybe. But it'll work out," Livi insisted, her smile only a little shaky around the edges. "Really, there's no need to worry."

Tessa almost threw the chocolates against the wall. What was it going to take to get Livi to show a little anger and act like herself again?

"Apparently there is reason to cry hysterically," Tessa pointed out acerbically. "I just left your mother bawling on your aunt's shoulder."

Livi opened her mouth, looking as if she were going to whitewash that with flowers and puppy dogs, too, so Tessa added, "Over a bottle of cheap rum."

"Oh." Livi grimaced. "That's bad. I'll have to find her and smooth it over."

"Oh, no." Tessa stepped sideways to block the door. "No more smoothing. You're smooth enough for everyone. Why don't you tell me what's going on instead."

After a quick frown at her blocked escape route, Livi shrugged and sat on the bed. Knowing how sneaky she could be, Tessa tossed the chocolates and tissues on a chair in case she needed her hands.

"Mitch just got word that his leave has been changed," Livi said, her voice hitching. "He's been assigned to some special mission. He won't tell me anything except that he has to report on Thursday."

Her worst fear confirmed, Tessa leaned against the door and shook her head.

"But you're getting married Saturday. They can't do that," Tessa said, ready to take on the US Navy.

"Yeah. They can." Livi shrugged. "What can I say? Duty trumps 'I do.'"

Tessa rubbed her hand over her mouth to keep from snapping *bullshit*. "What changed? I mean, he had the time approved. It was all arranged. How can they change it? Isn't his grandfather an admiral? Can't he pull strings?"

"Maybe. No. I don't know." Livi pushed her hands through her hair. "He said it's complicated. Apparently he wasn't even supposed to be on this mission but someone was pulled off the team. Then they changed the launch date or whatever he called it, but there isn't time to bring in someone else."

Tessa wanted to object.

She wanted to protest.

If it'd help, she'd bitch up a storm.

But she was pretty sure none of that would help and any of it would upset Livi. So she did the next best thing. She tried to think of a solution.

"Okay, then let's move the wedding up," she suggested desperately. "Get married tomorrow, or tonight even. I know it's not ideal, but at least you'll have a few days together."

For a second Livi's face lit up. But just as fast it dimmed again. Her shoulders drooped as she sighed.

"I couldn't." She shook her head. "People are expecting the ceremony on Saturday. Some of the guests aren't even here yet. We can't disappoint them."

Her voice trailed off, her expression crumbling a little before she plastered that damned smile on her face again.

Tessa couldn't help it.

She threw back her head and screamed.

She'd spent the past two months pretending to be something she wasn't—nice and agreeable. She'd kept her mouth shut instead of voicing her opinion so often that she'd been afraid she'd go mute. She'd put on a smile and played nice with people who drove her batty. All in an attempt to be the right kind of friend.

Well, screw that.

She opened her eyes, ready to tell Livi just what they were going to do to fix this mess.

But apparently she'd finally found a way to burst Livi's Zen bubble. Now, instead of looking mellow and content, tears waterfalled down her friend's face onto hands that were shaking too hard to open the tissue box.

"Oh, damn," Tessa muttered, her own bottom lip trembling. She rushed over to take the tissues, tearing the box in half in her haste. "Don't cry. Or, here, dry your face. We'll fix this."

"We can't," Livi wailed. "There's too much to change. Too many people will be pissed. Mitch and I will have to wait, marry later at city hall or something."

Oh, hell no. Tessa cringed. There had to be a way to fix this.

"It sucks." Livi sniffed, sounding like her old self for a moment. "After everything that went into the wedding, all the drama and putting up with my mother, now this happens? I've tried to stay positive and optimistic. I don't want the baby born with frown lines and a negative attitude."

Tessa blinked. Could that really happen? She didn't know enough to debate it, so she did the next best thing. She plopped down next to Livi and opened the box of chocolates.

After they'd each had a couple of pieces, she sighed.

"Will worry really mess up the baby's personality?"

"Maybe. After I read all of the pregnancy books I could find I started on old wives' tales. Just in case. I might have gone overboard a little." Livi rubbed her hand over the small bump and shrugged. "The doctor said now that I'm into my second trimester that there's less risk, but you know…"

Yeah. She wrapped her arm around Livi's slightly expanded waist. She knew.

Livi gave a watery sigh and dropped her head to rest on hers just as the door opened.

For one second, panic flashed in Super SEAL's eyes, then bless him, Mitch squared his shoulders and crossed the room to take his fiancée into his arms.

"Aww, sweetie, don't cry."

Tessa smiled.

He really was a nice guy. So perfect for Livi.

All of her doubts about their marriage and every worry

she'd had fled at the look on his face as he held her best friend.

She'd be damned if anything was going to ruin their wedding. Tessa set her chin and got to her feet.

"Here." She handed Mitch the candy and went for the door. "I've got some things I need to take care of."

She was finished trying to be the right kind of friend. Now she'd be the only kind she knew how.

A pain-in-the-butt know-it-all smart-ass with excellent taste, fabulous instincts and the ability to get things done.

All she needed was one thing to make it happen.

Gabriel.

GABRIEL STOOD ON the cliffs watching Mitch marry the woman he loved as the sun rose over the ocean behind them. His eyes cut from the happy couple, their faces glowing as they stared into each other's eyes, to Tessa. Like him, she was standing back from the couple, letting them take center stage with the minister.

He was a little stunned at how fast Tessa could make things happen. Barely twelve hours ago she'd pounded on his door demanding help. Somehow in that time she'd planned the ceremony, arranged for a wedding breakfast and rescheduled the honeymoon to begin that afternoon.

In other words, she'd cleaned up his mess.

His shoulders knotted with tension, Gabriel remembered his talk with the groom before the ceremony. Irish had insisted that he didn't blame Gabriel. He'd even tried to claim that he'd requested the assignment to make up for Jeglinski being a fuckup.

But Gabriel knew who the real fuckup was.

If he'd followed his own rules and kept the issue to himself instead of giving in to pressure, he wouldn't have disappointed the team or let down Irish.

Gabriel didn't mind paying the price for his decisions. But he'd be damned if others would, too.

Not his team. Not his best friend.

And no way in hell the woman he loved.

Which meant he needed to stick with his rules from now on. All of them.

Watching Tessa wipe a tear from her cheek as the bride and groom kissed, he knew letting her go was going to be the hardest thing he'd ever done. Dragging it out wouldn't make it any easier. Setting his jaw against the sight of Tessa's joy, he decided to leave right after the happy couple.

Two hours later, Gabriel had one eye on Irish, watching for the signal that he was heading out, and the other on the doors to make sure he had a clear escape route as soon as that happened. He wasn't proud of the fact, but he needed a little distance before he told Tessa they were through.

"Yo, Romeo. Whatcha doing in the corner?"

Since he wasn't about to admit that he was avoiding a woman, Gabriel shrugged instead.

"Just watching."

"Hell of a party, huh?" Lee Martin said. The team gunner was the size of a small bull, but managed to make the crystal flute of champagne look delicate in his beefy hand. "Pure class, ya know."

Just like the lady who'd planned it all. Gabriel looked around the dining room. From the sparkling crystal to the fabric-draped chairs, it shouted *fancy wedding*. And from the expression on the bride's face, it screamed *perfect*.

"There you are," Scavenger said, joining them. "Irish was looking for you. Said to make sure you didn't cut out."

"Why's Irish worried?" Martin asked. "It's not as if Romeo has ever left a party early. Unless it was on the arm of a beautiful woman, of course."

"You okay, dude?" Scavenger asked, ignoring Martin. "You're not taking this on, are you? You better not be."

"That's crap if you own this," Martin agreed, his broad face turning ruddy. "Jeglinski was a problem. I'm all for competition and wanting to be the best, but that guy had no regard for boundaries. No respect for the mission. You did right to report him."

"There were other ways to handle the situation" was all Gabriel said. "Better ways."

"Not with a guy like that. He wasn't gonna stop."

Martin's nod echoed Scavenger's words.

"Look, the mission date wasn't changed because of anything you did. That's just how it goes down. You know that," Scavenger said, his expression fierce. "And Irish choosing to go? You think he was going to trust this mission to anyone else after he realized what Jeglinski had been doing? He's got to safeguard the team. That's his job."

A job he wouldn't have had to do if Gabriel had handled things right. He didn't say that, though. He knew they weren't going to hear him. That was what team loyalty was all about. One man covering the other's ass.

"It is what it is," he said instead.

"Damned right it is," Martin said, slapping him on the back. "And what it is, is a win. Jackrabbit was bragging but you showed him. He's off the team, and when word gets back that you won the bet by hooking up with the gorgeous brunette, he's gonna curl up in a corner and cry like a baby." Martin's usually affable face turned to stone. "Small payment for trying to incapacitate you and ruining Irish's honeymoon, I say."

"Back off, Martin," Scavenger said quietly. "Just let it go."

"Let it go? No way, man. Romeo here is the king. He deserves to be honored, man. He took Jackrabbit down like a hunter bags his prey." The other man's face turned sly. "And what better reward than a sexy brunette who writes how-tos for sex games, right?"

"Actually, I write how-tos for flirting, but I suppose those are sex games in a way."

Gabriel figured it was a testament to how off-kilter he was that he hadn't sensed Tessa's approach. But it was almost worth being busted to see the look of shamed horror pour over Martin's face. His cheeks turned red, his lips went white and he hung his head so low Gabriel was surprised he wasn't looking backward through his belly button.

"Sorry, ma'am," Martin muttered, edging around her and scurrying away with impressive haste for a man his size.

A wicked smile played over her lips as Tessa watched him go. Then she looked back at Gabriel with one brow arched and a hint of anger in her eyes.

Scavenger glanced from one of them to the other, then mumbled an excuse and faded away.

Had she overheard? How much? A part of him hoped she'd heard enough to get seriously pissed, to realize that he was to blame for ruining Livi and Mitch's wedding. If she got pissed, she'd pick a fight, rightfully chew him out. Then he could simply walk away.

But that would be cowardly. And Gabriel hadn't been raised to be a coward.

Instead, he stood at ease and waited for the fallout.

"Have you been avoiding me?" The question wasn't the fallout he'd expected, though.

He frowned.

"Avoiding you? Why would I do that?"

"That's what I was wondering."

With her hair pulled back into a high ponytail and curls sweeping over one bare shoulder, she reminded him of a mythical goddess. Gold bracelets bracketed her from biceps to wrist, jewels sweeping her cheeks. The lack of sleep—and he knew she hadn't had any because she'd been working her ass off all night—didn't show.

She was damn near irresistible.

Good thing he was trained to do the impossible.

"Just watching the show," he said, using his chin to indicate the party going on behind her. "You did a good job."

She tossed a frown over her shoulder.

"Maybe. Everything happened so fast, I haven't had a chance to talk to Livi. I hope she's happy with it."

"Why wouldn't she be?"

"Ask the mother of the bride."

"Yeah, she's pretty messed up." Remembering the pale-faced, heavy-eyed woman who'd left the celebration early, Gabriel grimaced. "Is she really twisted that you changed things?"

"It could be the results of cheap rum." Tessa wrinkled her nose. "But I'm sure when the hangover wears off, she'll be ready to kick my butt."

"You saved her daughter's wedding. She'd do better to be kissing your butt."

"Now, there's an image I didn't need." Tessa's laugh faded as fast as it had come and she gave him a long, searching look.

"Was what they said true?" she asked quietly. "Is it because you reported some moron that Mitch had to take over the mission? Is that why the wedding had to be changed?"

Yep.

But claiming that aloud would only piss off Irish, so Gabriel shrugged instead.

Her eyes hardened into blue ice.

"And the rest?"

"The rest of what?" he asked, stalling. His gut clenched

with misery. He knew what he had to do. But damn, this wasn't easy.

"Did you bet on our having sex?" she asked baldly, the words dripping icicles. "Was our entire relationship, everything that happened, based on some macho game?"

Ignoring the tension ratcheting through his body, Gabriel kept his expression mellow and easy. He knew Tessa.

He knew how to play her.

He'd figured out how to reel her in, so it was a given that he knew how to push her away.

Instead of telling her the truth—that he'd never paid any attention to Jackrabbit's dumb-ass challenge to begin with—or trying to smooth things over, he offered a half smile and a shrug.

"C'mon, angel. You know I can never resist a challenge."

He felt lower than a slug when her eyes flashed with pain. But he steeled himself to ignore it. He wouldn't demean her intelligence, even in his own mind by claiming that this was for her own good.

But it was better for both of them to end things now.

He had a path to walk, one he'd set in place years ago. A path he'd vowed to walk alone. He'd already screwed up enough things by ignoring his vows. He wasn't going to screw up Tessa's life.

"So you're claiming that you actually bet on getting me into bed?" A hint of pain beneath the ice, Tessa gave him an arch look. "Didn't I offer you hot sex at the engagement party?"

Damn. Gabriel almost frowned but caught himself.

"Like I said, I can't resist a challenge."

She didn't move. She barely blinked. But he could see her reel back as though she'd been slapped. She shook her head, as if trying to deny his claim.

"Ask any of the team," he suggested quietly. "They'll tell you."

Her gaze shifted around the room as if she were debating which one to ask. Not doubting for a second that she'd take the question to every single one of them, Gabriel squared his shoulders. He didn't want this to get ugly. One of the things he'd always prided himself on was that no relationship he'd ever been in had ended in anger.

Then again, he was pretty sure this was his first actual relationship. So there went his pride.

Gabriel scowled when shouts and applause filled the room, then he realized it wasn't over his downfall. He flicked a glance over Tessa's shoulder.

"Looks as if the bride and groom are saying their goodbyes." He paused, then forced the words out. "I've got to report to base, so I'll say mine now, too."

Her eyes rounded, her quick intake of breath catching before she managed to exhale. He felt about as low as a slug and knew he deserved to be squashed like one.

He waited for the recriminations. He wouldn't blame her if she hauled off and slapped him. He deserved anything and everything she shot his way.

But Tessa never went the typical route.

"Well, I guess we're through, then," she said with a brittle smile. "I'm off to say goodbye to Livi. And you're off to the rest of your life. Good luck with that."

She gave a toss of her hair, turned and sauntered away without another look.

Gabriel watched her go. It took every bit of strength he had not to call her back.

His grandfather, in all his wisdom, had never promised that walking the right path would be easy. But he'd never indicated that it'd be hard enough to make Gabriel believe that hearts could actually break.

13

MENTAL-HEALTH DAYS were for indulging. They were for curling up in jammies, huddling under a blanket with cocoa and pretending the rest of the world didn't exist. That Tessa had been doing the same thing every day since last Tuesday, when she'd fled Catalina, was beside the point.

Mental-health days weren't for having to haul her stiff body off the couch while wearing her rattiest pajamas—granted, they were only deemed ratty because they weren't silk—with her hair blown out and her face puffy from a five-day crying binge.

But some stubborn pain in the neck kept leaning on her doorbell, leaving Tessa no choice. She peered through the peephole, then closed her swollen eyes and groaned.

She didn't want to do this. She really didn't.

But she knew she had no choice.

So with a deep breath, and a bright fake smile, she opened the door.

"You forgot this." Not waiting for a greeting, Livi lifted a small box, the pretty purple foil glinting in the light as she strode into the apartment. "Your maid-of-honor gift."

"Aren't you supposed to be reveling in the glow of your honeymoon?" Tessa asked, letting the door shut with a bang. "Not delivering packages?"

"Believe it or not, I'm perfectly capable of handling more than one thing at a time."

Uh-oh. Tessa knew that tone. It was Livi's rarely heard gonna-kick-some-butt tone. Figuring it was the safest route, Tessa planted her own butt on the relative safety of the couch.

"I never said otherwise," she pointed out once she was settled.

"No? Then maybe you can fill me in on why you shut me out." Tossing the gift aside with enough force that Tessa seriously hoped it wasn't breakable, Livi started pacing the room.

"I didn't shut you out." Exactly. "You had so much going on, I simply chose not to add to your stress level."

"But see, here's the thing," Livi said in a tone riddled with hurt. "You were so busy not stressing me out that you forgot that you're supposed to be my friend."

"Why would I worry about your stress if I wasn't your friend?" Tessa snapped, suddenly furious. For months she'd kept her mouth shut, tried to be supportive. And this was what she got for it?

"I don't know what that was," Livi said with a shrug, her expression just as angry as Tessa's. "All I know is that it belittled our years of real friendship, mocked what we're supposed to be to each other."

Her jaw sinking to her chest, Tessa muttered, "Why don't you just kick me in the face? It'd be easier to take."

"How do you think I feel?" Livi demanded, throwing her hands in the air. "Do you think I like hearing big news from other people? You'd think after all these years you'd care enough to tell me yourself."

Big news?

What was she talking about? Tessa would usually pace at this point but she was afraid if she got off the couch she'd be mowed down.

"Wait." One hand rubbing the throbbing pain between her eyebrows, Tessa lifted her other hand in the air. "This isn't about your wedding?"

"My wedding? Why would I be upset about that?" The confusion in her eyes didn't lighten Livi's scowl.

"Because I didn't speak up more? Because I let Pauline run roughshod all over you instead of letting you have the wedding you wanted?" Tessa puffed out a breath and let her hands fall to her lap. "Because I jumped in with both feet, rearranged your entire ceremony and ended up doing the exact same thing as Pauline, only worse because I didn't even tell you while I was doing it."

Midrecital of all Tessa's crimes, Livi stopped pacing. She stood in the middle of the living room, her hands planted on her hips and her expression shifting from confused to irritated and then on to angry.

"Why the hell wouldn't you tell me any of that?" Livi demanded, towering over her like an avenging Valkyrie. She was almost a foot taller than Tessa to start with and built like a chiseled statue, but it was the rounded belly poking out at her that held the strongest intimidation factor.

Angling her chin at a stubborn angle helped avoid looking at the accusing baby bump and let Tessa offer her haughtiest stare.

"Every time I tried, you said you were fine with Pauline's tyranny, remember? Added to that, stress could endanger your pregnancy. Besides, you really didn't seem to want my involvement since every single thing I had anything to do with you ended up changing."

Whether it was the stare or the mention of her pregnancy, Tessa didn't know. But the anger drained from Livi's face.

"You didn't seem that interested," the blonde murmured, dropping to the couch. She pushed one hand through her hair, then shifted to tuck one foot under her so she could angle her body toward Tessa. "Or maybe I was just so busy trying to keep from going crazy that I didn't pay attention."

With anyone else, Tessa would toss off a smart-ass remark, something cutting that echoed the hurt she felt. She pressed her lips tight, but couldn't hold on to enough anger to even glare. After all, this was Livi.

But without the anger, all that was left was the hurt.

Still pressing her lips tight, now to keep them from trembling, she took a deep breath while trying to figure out how to explain without adding any more pain to her friend's face.

"I didn't want to upset you," she admitted quietly. "You already had one person nagging at you. I figured another was more than you or the baby needed."

"And?" Livi prompted, the stubborn look on her face making it clear that she wanted it all.

Tessa sighed and gave it to her as gently as she could.

"You were busy planning to be a wife and mother. You changed Stripped Down Fitness to a workout style that I don't fit into. You're starting a new life that I don't seem to have a place in." Hating the hurt she could see her words causing, Tessa bit her lip before forcing herself to continue. "So much was going on. And I was—I am—thrilled for you. But I felt as if I was losing your friendship."

"I don't understand how that's possible." Livi shook her head, her face both perplexed and hurt. "We've been friends our entire adult lives. We work together. We play together. We were friends through my first wedding, lousy marriage and nasty divorce. Why wouldn't we stay friends through my happy marriage, morning sickness and motherhood?"

Tessa had no answer to that, so she settled on a shrug.

"If you weren't upset about the wedding stuff, what did

you come here to bitch me out about?" she asked. Had Livi found out that Gabriel had dumped her?

"Your job."

Oh.

"Maeve stopped by this morning," Livi continued, her fingers tapping an aggravated beat on the arm of the couch. "Imagine my surprise when, along with the clever music box she brought for the baby, she shared her worry over your holing up here in your apartment."

That sank into Tessa's belly with a greasy thud.

"I guess I didn't say much about what was going on with *Flirtatious*," she admitted. Before she could offer up an excuse, Livi growled like a rabid mother bear.

"Much?" Livi repeated, showing that for all her sweet demeanor, she could do smart-ass with the best of them. "You mean much, like the fact that you sold your company? Much, like letting me in on how upset you must have been to give up something you've spent years building? Or maybe sharing what you're going to do next?"

"I should have told you," Tessa said with a wince.

"You should have trusted me," Livi amended.

"Trusted you? How do you figure that?"

"If you trusted me, you'd have faith in me. Not just in my being capable of juggling wedding drama, but in my being strong enough to listen to your worries without falling apart. You'd trust me to be your sounding board while you worked out your job issues and you'd know I'd have your back if you ran into trouble." Each word grew sharper until Livi's tone cut like a knife. "That's what trust is."

"I trust you," Tessa protested. "I was simply protecting you. That's what friends do, isn't it?"

"No," Livi said, her expression not softening an iota. "You were protecting you. Why?"

Tessa knew her bottom lip was drooping, but she

couldn't help it. There was nothing pretty about having the truth rubbed in her face.

"I didn't want you to know what a fraud I was," she finally admitted, the words tearing out of her in a painful rush. "I'm supposed to be so savvy and clever, with my finger on the pulse of all things sexy. But I haven't been to a club in months. I'm so bored with the singles scene. I used to love writing and now I have to bribe myself with the promise of new shoes to meet each deadline."

"Tessa, you've been doing this for a long time. You're bound to burn out on it."

"Do you ever burn out on fitness?"

"I would if I did the same workout all the time." Livi rubbed her hand over Tessa's knee. "Look, I know what you do is more than a job, it's how you define yourself. I do that, too. But if you're going to use that as a yardstick, you need to count the good stuff and not just the bad. You're damned good at what you do and you've built an excellent reputation doing it."

"It wasn't just my job I felt like a fraud at," she admitted, barely above a whisper, as she looked at her hands.

"You're not going to spout some crazy idea about feeling as if you weren't a good friend again, are you?" Livi asked, that sharp edge in her tone once more. "Because if you do I'm going to have to claim that I'm a selfish one since I was too self-absorbed to realize everything you were going through. And you don't want to make me admit that. I'll feel bad and probably give the baby wrinkles."

Tessa looked up with a watery laugh.

"Thanks." Tessa leaned over to give Livi a hug. She might not be a fraud, but she was damned lucky. It didn't matter if she easily fit into the mold she'd carefully designed for herself any longer. What mattered was the reason why.

Because she'd grown. As a person, as a writer, even as a friend. And her world was bigger now because of it.

"So," Livi said after a few healing minutes, "want to fill me in on all of those worries you have over my marriage?"

"Why don't I do you one better," Tessa said with a deep breath and the mental image of diving off a cliff. "Why don't I fill you in on all of my worries over falling in love with Gabriel."

"Love? You're using the *love* word? Oh, my God." Livi clapped her hands, her face lit with joy. "Wait? You and Gabriel? Hang on, we need chocolate for this."

By the time they'd devoured Tessa's sadly depleted stash of cookies, Livi had heard the whole story and Tessa felt more like herself than she had in months.

Especially when Livi's eyes narrowed with indignant fury on her behalf.

"You let him get away with that? Just, what? Let him walk?"

"Well, what was I supposed to do?" Tessa scowled. "Tie him up and make him my love slave? I think there are rules against that."

"You were supposed to do what you'd tell anyone else to. Call him on the bullshit and force him to be honest about what was going on. Holy crap, Tess, even I would do that much." Livi shook a cookie at her. "But you pushed him away instead. You let him get away with it because you were scared. You were protecting yourself again."

Tessa tried to respond, but the chocolate chips had turned to sawdust in her mouth. Livi took advantage by snagging the last cookie.

Had she let him push her away?

Tessa pressed her finger against the cookie crumbs left on the plate, realizing that she'd been so busy thinking that she was a fraud at things she was great at, she'd figured there was no chance she wouldn't be one at something she'd never thought she'd be good at. Then she gave Livi a glum look.

"You're right. I blew it. What am I supposed to do now?" she asked, for the first time in her life lost on how to handle a situation with the opposite sex. "He pushed me away for a reason. What's the point in calling him on it?"

"The point comes down to what you want. Do you want to make him pay for hurting you? Or do you want to make him see that the two of you are perfect for each other?"

GABRIEL STEPPED OFF the elevator to Mitch and Livi's apartment, the memory of the last time he'd been here flooding him with a needy sort of pleasure.

With the same narrow focus and determination that got him through brutal workouts and ugly battles, he shoved that memory right back out of his mind. It'd been two weeks since he'd last seen Tessa, though, and his theory that it'd get easier with time was proving to be complete crap. Instead of fading from his memory, her image was growing sharper, the need for her more edgy and pronounced.

Put it aside, he ordered himself as he approached the apartment door. He and Irish were back on an even keel, the other man insisting that everything was fine. Even the mission had gone well. Gabriel figured that was what tonight was. A friendly dinner invitation to prove that everything was copacetic.

But while Irish might have absolved him of the guilt of ruining his wedding, Gabriel hadn't forgiven himself for putting the team in jeopardy. Since he knew that fact just irritated the other man, he'd been putting on his friendliest face, pretending everything was cool. Things like showing up at Irish's instead of copping a much-needed nap in the barracks.

"Reporting as ordered," he said, throwing Irish a salute when the other man opened the door.

"Smart-ass remarks won't help," Irish told him, stepping back to gesture him inside. "Actually, I'm going to wish you luck because I'm not sure there's any help for you now."

"You're cooking dinner?" Gabriel frowned. "Couldn't we just do takeout?"

"Oh, now, that'd just be mean," Livi said, joining them in the entryway. From the look on her face, she hadn't gotten the copacetic memo. Either that, or she'd talked to Tessa.

"For you," Gabriel said, handing her a bouquet of flowers. He'd gone for the extralarge one, but stopped short of buying chocolates. He wanted to apologize, not kiss ass.

"How lovely," she said in the same tone she'd probably use if he'd handed her a bag of snails.

Gabriel glanced at Irish, who offered a slight shrug.

Yeah. Livi and Tessa had been talking.

Picturing a very cool evening ahead, Gabriel wished he'd worn long sleeves.

Then Livi tucked the bouquet under one arm and her purse under the other.

"Go on in," Irish invited. "Drinks and food are on the table."

"Where are you going?" Confused, he watched as Irish and Livi stepped around him to get to the door.

"There are things I just don't want to see," Irish said, opening the door for his wife.

"Good luck," Livi added with a chilly smile just before it shut in Gabriel's face.

Damn.

Gabriel closed his eyes, barely resisting the urge to follow them out. But knowing his CO, Irish would be waiting in the hallway to make sure he didn't do just that.

Knowing what was waiting for him, Gabriel squared his shoulders, smoothed his expression into something hopefully close to dignified and did an about-face for the living area.

"Hello, angel," he greeted with an easy smile when he stepped into the room. "This is a surprise."

A damned good-looking one. Being a woman who knew how to make the most of what she had—and more, one who knew just where to stick a knife—Tessa had pulled out all the stops tonight.

She hadn't gone for a revealing dress that screamed sex like some women would have. No, his angel was too smart for that.

Instead, she was wearing a simple black skirt that ended midknee. She'd paired it with an off-the-shoulder T-shirt depicting a skull wearing lipstick that revealed a black tank underneath. Short ankle boots completed her battle gear.

That she was ready for battle was a given.

The only question was, what was her objective?

To make him suffer was a given. But she'd have achieved that with their friends present. So she had bigger aims.

"Did you miss me?" he teased, hoping to irritate her enough that she'd show her hand. Because the sooner he figured it out, the sooner he could end the torture of seeing her and not being able to touch, not being able to taste.

"Were you gone?" she teased, tilting her head to the side so her long curls skimmed over one breast. Gabriel's chest—and other things—constricted. Before he could reply, or even find the breath to consider it, she waved her hand toward the table next to her. "Drink? Something to eat?"

"No, thanks."

"You really should try something," she told him, taking a small plate of appetizers and a glass of wine with her as she moved to the couch. "It's excellent. Livi went all out. I think she's trying to appease her guilt over her part in this evening's fun."

Gabriel rocked back on his heels, impressed with her strategy. She wasn't even going to pretend that this wasn't an ambush. So maybe he shouldn't bother pretending he was okay with it.

"What's the deal?" he asked.

"The deal? Oh, that'd be the unfinished business between us," she said, shifting so her skirt slid up her leg just a little. Gabriel considered it a credit to his willpower that he didn't lick his lips.

"I thought we wrapped it up pretty well," he said. "Unless you wanted to get in a few digs about that bet? Or collect on the winnings?"

Figuring that'd piss her off, he steeled himself for the lash of temper.

But Tessa just laughed.

"Silly Romeo," she chided with a wicked laugh. "I'm an expert at games between the sexes, remember? Did you really think that little ruse would work on me?"

Well, yeah.

"I'll admit, I was surprised to find out about your part in the wedding changes," she admitted slowly, tapping her finger against her lips as if she was considering her next words. Or just reminding him of how kissably delicious her mouth was. "But only because you hadn't mentioned it while doing everything in your power to help me pull off the ultimate wedding rescue. You did bust your butt helping out after all. Even calling in favors to get a helicopter that'd fly you to the mainland at night, waking vendors, bribing store clerks."

Gabriel shifted, all but shuffling his feet as he tried to dismiss her words. Harder to ignore was the look of admiration on her face, though.

"You did all the heavy lifting," he said dismissively. "I just followed orders."

"Right. Orders. That's what caused the problem that led to the wedding changes, isn't it?" At his scowl, she rolled her eyes. "Don't get your boxers in a twist. Mitch didn't spill any secrets. All he said was that you'd followed orders. Which is good, since that's what you're supposed to do, isn't it? He also mentioned that the mission changed, that the team would have had to go regardless."

"He wouldn't have."

"And that is between you and Mitch," she said with a shrug. "It's impossible for me to argue with confidential information. But knowing the both of you, I can surmise that he did exactly what he thought he had to, just like you did. Since you both have that Boy Scout gene going, I'm sure in both cases it was for the good of the team."

Gabriel wanted to explain why she was wrong. He wanted to point out the missteps he'd made, the potential problems he'd caused. But he had a feeling she'd react the same way Irish had. By telling him to get over himself.

"What's between you and me, on the other hand, had nothing to do with the good of anybody." Her voice shifted from reasonable to cold with a flick of those lush lashes. "And for that, you do owe me an explanation."

"Will you accept it if I offer one?" he challenged.

"Of course."

Yeah, right. Gabriel knew better, but he also knew that she was right. He owed her more than a brush-off.

"One of the team was gunning to take me down and I

kept ignoring him. He pulled a lot of stupid stunts, trying to trip me up. I finally reported him, which is why Irish had to step in to take his place on the mission."

"And how is this a reason to dump me?" she asked in that same reasonable tone that was driving him crazy.

"I was too distracted by what was happening between us to pay attention," he snapped. "If I'd been focused like I should have been, I'd have seen that the guy wasn't going to throttle back. I'd have taken steps before things got out of hand."

"Must suck, seeing the best in people," she mused. "You do it all the time, you know. Your teammates. This idiot with a chip on his shoulder. Me. You're not blind to the possibilities, Gabriel. You just choose to believe the best." She slowly rose, her eyes not leaving his as she crossed the room. "How come you can't see the same in yourself?"

"Please. I don't have ego issues," he said with a hoarse laugh. His hands twitched with need, desperate to touch her. But he knew he was teetering on the edge so he held firm.

"No, you have an amazingly healthy ego," she agreed. Her hands, apparently, had no rules about touching because she chose that moment to press them to his chest. "But you seem to think you have to walk this narrow line and that one misstep on either side deserves punishment."

"Not punishment," he denied, trying to ignore how right, how wonderfully right, her hands felt on his body. "Just accounted for."

"Was that what you were doing when you blew me off after the wedding?" she asked quietly. "Accounting for your feelings for me because you blame them for your thinking everyone was a team player like you?"

How did she do that? She'd neatly twisted it all around as if he wasn't to blame for what had happened. She'd probably done it the same way she'd worked it out so his hands were gripping her waist despite his intentions not to touch.

"You were right about me," she told him, the confident mask falling away to show the sweet vulnerability beneath. "I was so worried about my image that I lost myself. I let my reputation as a man-eating vamp convince me that we had no chance of anything beyond hot sex."

"You're not your reputation," he said, irritated to see her dismiss herself so easily.

"No?" She smiled a wicked little smile. "Well, then, if I'm not, and if you were right about my letting those worries define me, then you must have been right about the other thing."

Gabriel knew a trap when he heard it. He knew that if he didn't sidestep, he'd be caught good and solid. But she felt so good in his hands. He felt so good just being with her. So he didn't care. He walked, eyes wide-open, into the trap.

"What other thing?"

"That you and I are so hooked on our images, our reputations, that we're afraid to make changes. Even when not making changes means giving up the person we love."

Oh, shit.

Had she really said that?

There was a roaring in his ears, but Gabriel was pretty sure she had. Not just because her eyes were huge and vulnerable, but because his heart felt whole for the first time in his life.

His brain threw up caution signs, though, warning him to step carefully. A fall at this point would be treacherous for both of them.

"You know if we do this relationship it's not going to be easy, right?" he warned. "I'm a SEAL. I'm gone a lot of the time. I'll never be able to tell you everything I'm doing, everywhere I am."

"I know," she said, the teasing light in her eyes fading as she grew serious. "My best friend married a SEAL, remember? I spent a lot of time asking myself how she could do it, how she could deal with it. But now I know."

"You do?"

"She loves him." Tessa shrugged. "Which is why I know I can handle it, too. Because I really do love you."

Finally letting himself believe that he could really walk this path with Tessa at his side, Gabriel rested his forehead against hers as he whispered, "I love you, too."

"Forever?"

"Forever," he agreed.

All it took was a little hop for Tessa to wrap her legs around his waist. Her hands locked behind his neck, she winked and gestured toward the couch.

"Why don't we get started, then?"

"It'll be my pleasure," he promised.

* * * * *

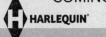
COMING NEXT MONTH FROM

Available May 19, 2015

#847 MIDNIGHT THUNDER
Thunder Mountain Brotherhood
by Vicki Lewis Thompson

An emergency may have brought wandering cowboy
Cade Gallagher home, but the heat between him and former
flame Lexi Simmons is enough to keep him there. Lexi
isn't sure she trusts him, but she can't help give in to the
intense attraction...

#848 Fevered Nights
Uniformly Hot!
by Jillian Burns

Supermodel Piper Metcalf is trying to reform her bad-girl ways.
Just her luck she's met the only good guy who's trying to be
bad—sexy SEAL Neil Barrow. Will he be the one temptation she
can't turn down?

#849 COME ON OVER
Made in Montana
by Debbi Rawlins

Shelby Foster arrives at her inherited ranch desperate for a
fresh start. Too bad the Montana spread already has an
owner—seriously hot horse trainer Trent Kimball—and he is
not impressed!

#850 TRIPLE TIME
The Art of Seduction
by Regina Kyle

Straitlaced DA Gabe Nelson needs a friendlier image, and
bartender/artist Devin Padilla is happy to help him shake things
up. But their relationship turns more than friendly *fast*, and
opposites don't just attract—they get downright scorching.

**YOU CAN FIND MORE INFORMATION ON UPCOMING HARLEQUIN® TITLES,
FREE EXCERPTS AND MORE AT WWW.HARLEQUIN.COM.**

HBCNM0515